About the author

I obtained a law degree from King's College which I promptly traded in for a twenty year corporate career.

I resigned my post to start my own business in telecoms and ten years later was in the fortunate position of being able to retire. So I did.

And retirement has allowed me the time to develop my novel writing ambitions, the latest of which is *Gaslight*.

This is the first in a series of detective stories involving Sam Cove and his constant battle with his own integrity and morality.

GASLIGHT

Ben Bridle

GASLIGHT

Vanguard Press

A CIP catalogue record for this title is
available from the British Library.

ISBN 978-1-80016-446-8

Vanguard Press is an imprint of
Pegasus Elliot Mackenzie Publishers Ltd.
www.pegasuspublishers.com

First Published in 2023

Vanguard Press
Sheraton House Castle Park
Cambridge England

Printed & Bound in Great Britain

CHAPTER ONE

I didn't care what he said, nobody survived a fall from that height.

Her large, crumpled body lay flat on the pavement, her dark ruby blood oozing out from underneath, creeping across the flagstones, draining away and down into the kerbside gutter.

She was completely motionless. Still.

I'd seen more life on a butcher's block.

In fairness the paramedic kneeling over her seemed confident, almost insistent she'd pull through, if only they got her into the ambulance and off to hospital in time. But I very much doubted it.

And I wondered whether that crowd of agitated voyeurs saw things the same way as him. Because if they did they weren't helping much, resisting his repeated pleas no matter how many times he begged them to back off and give him space.

I looked up at the red brick apartment block towering over us and then back down at her. The ten-inch steel kitchen knife was plain for all to see, spilled onto the street by her side. But that wasn't what killed her. Dropping from nine storeys up there onto the cold concrete down here was plenty reason enough. Broken bones poking through flesh everywhere. Contorted limbs at strange angles as a result of her headlong fall. The pool of blood gathering under her head, running between the cracks in the pavement.

I pushed back against the large circle of onlookers pressed tight round that twisted, lifeless corpse. It was suffocating as I stepped away from the jostling crowd so fascinated by the frantic triage happening right in front of them.

My mood matched the cold, dank, grey Monday morning. As I left the scene and trudged wearily across the street I saw two more ambulances and a fleet of police cars screaming toward the incident. They had less than no chance of assisting unless they were prepared to mow down the assembled masses.

I pulled my coat collar up against the bitter cold. The chill morning breeze washed over my face and I wondered what the rest of this distressing day would bring.

Because I knew that woman. And her family. Just like I knew the apartment block standing over her, stone cold to her fate.

CHAPTER TWO

Back in the safety of my shabby fifth floor office I poured myself a mug of yesterday's tepid coffee, went to the window, pulled the wooden slats apart and looked back down the to the far end of the street where the onlookers were still gathered.

The police had created a cordon to help the paramedics move the body. I watched on transfixed as they slid her shattered body onto the ambulance trolley and then into the back of the mobile hospital. Then they sped away, electronic bells clanging, sirens shrieking, eternally hopeful that today their efforts might make a difference but knowing deep down that they probably wouldn't.

I turned my back on the carnage and slumped in my stained leather captain's chair behind my stained leather roll top desk. I drained the last dregs of coffee out of my ring-stained coffee cup.

Staring at the wall across the room my private investigator credentials still looked pretty impressive, embossed in parchment and captured forever under cover of glass. So that's what I did for a living was it? Well maybe.

My thoughts turned to the broken woman and what little I knew of her broken life.

CHAPTER THREE

A week earlier that woman's sister had stormed into my office, ignoring Maggie's frantic pleas. She covered the ground between the ante room and my office desk with an elegant grace and deceptive speed. Sleek. Dangerous. In fairness to Maggie she had no chance of saving me. After all she was paid to be my secretary, not my bodyguard. Though sometimes I thought she got slightly confused.

Anyway, who the hell cared? I definitely didn't need protecting from the vision that had just stepped into my world.

She was in her early thirties, blonde shoulder length curled hair, pale pink skin. Wearing a pink silk collarless blouse above a slim fit brown pencil skirt covering her tanned legs down to the knee. And she was sporting three-inch tan court shoes just for good measure.

But that wasn't it. Not at all.

It was her eyes... They were azure blue and on fire, a chilling blue flame burning bright. They set her porcelain face ablaze with their anger; her rich red lips trembling, struggling to keep her emotions at bay as she stood poised, legs astride in front of my desk staring darkly at me.

By the looks of things I thought I might be in trouble. And it didn't take long to find out.

"Sam Cove?"

Hardly a revelation, the name was peeling off my glass panelled office door for everyone to see.

I nodded in recognition and waved Maggie away. I sat very still, waiting.

"You owe me two grand." The words were choking her as she spat them out with real venom.

And finally there she was, my mystery Mercedes convertible owner, at last identified and flushed out.

We shared the same apartment block in Chelsea. She'd used one of my two reserved parking spaces for the last time last night. I would have no more. She'd left her soft top down so I'd taken retribution by emptying the contents of my green waste bin into her car.

In fairness I'd placed my business card on her leather dashboard for identification purposes. I thought it would get her attention and it obviously had.

"Why do I owe you money?" Like I didn't know.

"You fucking imbecile...that's what it'll cost me to clean up your mess!"

Hmm...very expressive and a tad excessive at the same time. But she was so devastatingly attractive in this frenzy of anger and frustration that she was going to get away with most things in her life, including a docker's turn of phrase. I called for backup.

"Maggie, coffee please. Would you care to join me Miss... sorry, I didn't quite catch your name?

Was that steam coming out of her ears?

She leaned over the desk, grabbed my ink bottle and crashed it down so hard the contents spewed all over my ink blotter, splashing her pink silk shirt at the same time. What a pity, that was such a pretty colour. But the simple truth was she was never going to get the black Quink out of that fine cloth now.

I knew I shouldn't laugh, but I wasn't that disciplined. I put my head down trying to conceal my chuckles but my shaking shoulders gave the game away.

I looked up just in time to take evasive action as the rest of the ink pot sailed past my head, crashing into a thousand pieces on the wall behind me.

"So no to the coffee then?" I shouted after her as she ran out, leaving her screaming abuse trailing behind her as she went.

CHAPTER FOUR

Maggie was there in a moment, coffee in one hand, cleaning agents in the other, giggling as she walked through.

I pulled myself together, ran around the desk and set off in pursuit of my mysterious potty mouthed beauty.

I caught her at the lifts and pulled up short, wary of the possibility of another salvo coming my way. I put my hands up by way of surrender.

"I still don't know your name and you definitely know mine. Kind of unfair, don't you think?"

I offered her my silk handkerchief, ostensibly so she could clean herself up, but in reality I just wanted to see her pert little breasts jiggling as she tried to wipe some of that black ink stain out. I was that shallow.

There was a massive silence during which the lift came and went while she carried on dabbing and smearing the ink all over her front.

I felt myself starting to laugh again but thankfully she interrupted me.

"Heather Scott. And you still owe me two grand."

That cold fire was still in her eyes, but it was smouldering now and so was I as I looked at her properly for the first time.

I saw her faint smile as she recognised the absurdity of our situation and something deep down inside me stirred. The feeling was new to me. I may have caught my breath. I put my hand inside my back pocket, retrieved my wallet and pulled out my calling card.

"Well Heather Scott if you want reparations you'd better be nicer to me. Much nicer. Here's another card. Give me a call when you've had a chance to clean up. I think I can stretch to a Starbucks."

I turned and walked back to my office, praying she was still watching me, but pretty sure she wasn't.

CHAPTER FIVE

She called at lunchtime to reintroduce herself and to apologise.

"Hello Mr Cove, it's the Quink girl. No weapons on me this time, only an apology for my behaviour and the offer to make up with that coffee you suggested this morning."

"Hi Heather. It's Sam by the way. So where and when?"

We arranged to meet in the Blue Bird at twelve thirty. I went home and changed into jeans, brown sheepskin jacket and soft Gucci loafers. I was definitely dressing to impress the Quink girl. I got to the restaurant fashionably early at midday and spent the next half hour rehearsing my opening lines.

I'd decided on some cool shit about her poor aim and her flagrant disregard for other people's property, but when I saw her in the hallway all that was forgotten, along with any sense of who or where I was.

All she'd done was change her top, the ink-stained pink silk affair replaced by the same in blue, precisely matching her piercing eyes. But what a difference it made. I stood up and went to greet her with a handshake and a polite kiss on either cheek. We returned to my seating area. I was inquisitive.

"How come people like you can get away with that?"

She looked puzzled as she sat down and crossed her slim brown legs.

"Get away with what?" she smiled.

"A simple change of top and a completely new attitude to match."

She looked agitated again. "You literally trashed my Mercedes. Not funny. And you laughed at me in your office; not funny at all. If you didn't care for my parking habits you might have mentioned it before treating my car like your own personal skip."

She had a point, but if I'd done that then I probably wouldn't be sitting here with her right now, would I?

"Fair enough. I'm sorry. Would you like that coffee? Columbian, or perhaps something more exotic?"

The apology came naturally. I've had enough practice doing it over my past thirty-five years on the planet.

She settled for a cappuccino and I settled back in my seat to admire the view.

"Sam, your card says you're a private investigator, so how long have you been practising?"

Great question.

How the hell had I ended up here, divorced, broke and living off other people's failures?

I looked up and met her level stare.

"I'm really not quite sure. I think it's a vocation. I just want to help people and make the world a better place. That and the fact that I'm broke and no one will give me a proper job."

Not exactly my life story, but enough to sidestep her question for now.

"Well I hope you make enough to pay for a valet?" She was obviously playing with me, so I knew I was forgiven.

"Just send me the bill."

The next hour flashed by. We talked about everything and nothing. It turned out she was a social influencer along with the rest of her family. They had over a million followers apparently. Bit like baby Kardashians. When I heard that news I really hoped my eyes didn't glaze over, because I had no idea what the hell she was talking about. She may as well have been describing the eating habits of the last tribes of the Incas for all I knew. So I just nodded at what seemed to be the appropriate moments and sooner or later the torture was over.

She seemed very interested in finding out more about me and my background though. Unfortunately for her I was equally interested in it remaining private. That said, the coffees came and went as she told me about her dysfunctional family, her brother and sister, her divorced parents, her failed relationships, in fact a lot of stuff I didn't expect her to open up about over coffee. But she wasn't giving much away; all of it was reported, regurgitated, recycled and updated hour by turgid hour on Facebook. That's how she made her money, living her life in the public eye.

Eventually it was time to let the real world back in. The talking was over and so was the coffee. We left the Blue Bird, politely kissed each other goodbye and went our separate ways.

And all the way back to the office I recreated our last few moments together. But this time I invented several different and perfectly natural chat lines I might have used to get to see her again.

And kicked myself for having failed because I was a dull sloth with no imagination or charisma.

CHAPTER SIX

But I'd no sooner stepped back into my musty office than Maggie thrust a note in my hands, muttering something about a mystery caller.

All she gave me was a scratchy piece of paper with a number on it. No name, nothing else. And then just as she had appeared, Maggie disappeared again without any explanations, almost as if by magic... I'd long thought she was a disciple of the dark arts.

I sat down and dialled the number. But as I began introducing myself I was immediately interrupted by a high pitched voice on the other end of the line.

"Hello Mr Cove and thanks for getting back to me so quickly. My name is Felicity Scott and I'm Heather's sister, you know, Heather Scott and she's just told me about you and what you do, so I called because I need you to look into something for me, you see I think I'm being followed, I can't swear to it but I keep getting the feeling there's someone behind me but then when I look round there's never anyone there, then the other day I saw a man's reflection in a shop window as I walked along the street and I think I might have seen him before but I'm not sure and it's got me wondering why someone would want to follow me and I'm worried I might have been mistaken for someone else, so I want you to look into it for me, would you?"

Some introduction. But she had to come up for air sooner or later, and while she was sucking it in I took my chance.

"Hi, Felicity. So you're Heather's sister are you? And are you as attractive as her too? Her twin maybe?"

There was a silence at the other end of the phone while she composed herself and considered her response.

"Well I really don't know what you mean Mr Cove. I don't know you at all and I only called because H said, but if you don't mind me saying, I don't like your tone Mr Cove, I really don't. So if you're not interested in finding my stalker then that's all right with me but you should just say so and not go asking personal questions that I have no intention of answering. And no I'm not her twin. Just her younger sister."

She went for another lung filler. I knew I only had a brief moment to respond.

"Pity. Felicity, are you available this afternoon?"

It took five minutes of my life and an all-out assault on my senses before she eventually agreed to come over. The meeting was set for three that afternoon.

I had no idea what had just happened, but I felt like I'd been ambushed by the Verbal Assault Squad.

And she was coming back this afternoon to dish out some more.

I couldn't wait.

CHAPTER SEVEN

Unsurprisingly, Felicity's shadow appeared in the frosted glass door which separated Maggie's ante room from mine at precisely three o'clock. I knew, because I was busy throwing scrunched up magazine spitballs at the wall clock when I saw her. It was an important moment; I was in the final of the World Darts play-offs with three shots for a glorious win. All I had to do was to hit the two, the six and the nine on that clock face and I was headed for darts immortality.

I reluctantly slid my feet off my desk and swept my spitballs off my clock as she was ushered in. As Maggie left the room she looked back at me with an enquiring eye. I knew why.

There was no way this lumpy sack of shit could have anything genetically to do with Heather.

For a start she must have weighed at least fifteen stones; two hundred and ten fat fleshy pounds all wrapped up in a pair of jeggings and a tight sports tank top. Like so much sausage meat forced into a wafer-thin skin of material constantly in danger of splitting wide open at any moment. She gripped her accompanying gym bag like it was her passport to freedom from her fat induced prison if only she could work out after our meeting,

It was deeply unsettling. I looked away and back into Maggie's office sanctuary for help. Strangely enough she was nowhere to be seen.

I turned back to Felicity, this time concentrating on her pudgy pudding face, trying not to see anything else.

"Hello… Ms Scott? Please come in and take a chair."

I gestured to the one across from my desk and she dutifully obliged. I was going to need a bigger chair. And I didn't have one. It groaned in disbelief as she settled into it.

"So tell me about your stalker."

Twenty minutes later I thought I had a rough idea about what was going on in Felicity's life.

Enough to know I wasn't interested in any part of it.

CHAPTER EIGHT

Twenty-nine, single and most likely still a virgin, Felicity's dull uneventful life as a nanny had recently changed irrevocably when she'd become somehow aware that she was being followed. Nothing specific, just shadows on walls, reflections in shop windows, house noises in the dead of night, that sort of thing.

Her recollection of events, like everything else about her, was so excruciatingly dull and so mind- blowingly tedious that eventually I had to take matters in hand. It was difficult to believe anything she said because nobody in their right mind would want to stalk her.

"So Felicity, what does this admirer look like? Is he sporting a thick brimmed trilby and a wide double-breasted suit? Or is he living in the shadows, hidden under his outsize tweed overcoat? Maybe he's gone for the dressed down look with leather jacket and jeans? Is he armed? Perhaps he's packing a machine gun for dramatic effect?"

I sat back and waited for the sarcasm to sink in. Eventually it fought its way through the blubber as she realised I was mocking her.

She stood up abruptly.

"How dare you Mr Cove! I came here in all good faith on the advice of my sister who suggested you might be able to help and all I've got is an insulting tone and what can only be described as barely disguised contempt for my quite rational fears that I might become the victim of some ne'er do well waiting in the shadows to do me in! If he sends me any more notes I don't know what I'm going to do because the police won't help, I've already tried and they say they can't do anything unless he breaks the law and sending threatening notes doesn't constitute a crime. Well it does in my book and I'm going to find someone who will help me even if you won't. Goodbye My Cove!"

And with that she turned on her heel, giving a passable impression of an enormous duck as she waddled towards the door.

But hold up. What notes? She hadn't mentioned any notes before, or if she had I was self-isolating, induced into a trance brought on by her dull expressionless monotones.

"Wait Ms Scott. Just take a seat and tell me about the correspondence you've received."

She stopped in her tracks, paused then turned back. Reaching into her voluminous bag she pulled out several pieces of crumpled paper and handed them to me. She sat down again. And the seat groaned again. I flattened the papers on my desk so I could read the hand written scrawl. It seemed somehow appropriate since she'd tried to flatten my seat...twice. The first of the three notes was very short and to the point.

'You think you're getting away with it don't you, you filthy pimp.'

Not much to go on. The second was even less helpful.

'What about the children?'

And then the final scrap of paper, 'You will have to pay.'

That wasn't really much at all, but my interest was well and truly piqued.

"When did you get these?"

She sat on the edge of my office chair, knees clasped together, clutching her leather gym bag. She suddenly looked very small and very scared. Her natural timidity overwhelmed by her fears for her own security.

"Well Mr Cove, I got the first one hand delivered through my letter box a couple of days ago. The second came in the regular post the day before yesterday. The last one was hand delivered to my place of work this morning and left at reception. I'm frightened Mr Cove. How does he know me, where I live, where I work? What does he want?"

It suddenly struck me that she might actually feel afraid, alone. That this was very real to her and very unnerving.

But I had another image of her stuck in my mind too and I couldn't shake it. It was of her sweaty, slippy, shiny fat body slowly rising up and down on her cross-trainer, pumping those pedals for all she was worth, shouting her defiance at an uncaring world. Completely oblivious to anything or anyone in her immediate proximity. Totally vulnerable, yet entirely unaware of any danger around her.

I made a decision.

"Okay Felicity, try not to worry. I'll look into it and get back to you."

We swapped contact details and said our goodbyes, but as she left I was reaching for my jacket to follow.

After all my in tray wasn't exactly brimming with exciting detective work. Or any work at all in fact. Not even any seedy matrimonial kiss and tell to investigate. All that was stopping me following Felicity was that spitball darts play off with the wall clock.

It chimed four times to signal the hour and I should have taken it as a sign, sat right back down and finished my match.

As it was, I headed out of the office, thereby adding that to the ever growing list of things I should have done to make my life easier but hadn't.

CHAPTER NINE

Flick humped her body on board a bus on the King's Road and it headed on up towards Sloane Square. I ran downstairs to my sexy sixties' soft top apple green Beetle, affectionately named Betty and set off in stop-start pursuit. When the bus stopped in Victoria she stepped off, crossing over the road to her gym. I'm sure I saw the bus suspension on the backplate lift a couple of inches in relief. I knew it was a gym because of the legend on the wall trailing what was inside: 'GYMBOTICS'. Roughly translated it meant a lifetime's boredom and penury, a monument to the myth that fitness means beauty and high self-esteem. I parked up close by.

I didn't have a gym pass but then I didn't need one; the owners had kindly provided a glass walled gallery on the first floor so potential members could look down on what they were missing. I leaned against the handrail as Felicity entered the gym. And what a sight she was. Still wearing the clothing she had on in my office, still armed with her kitbag, but now cradling a personalised water bottle for company. As she limbered up I felt that slightly nauseous feeling you get just before throwing up. So much flesh and most of it moving in isolation from the rest of its supposed muscle groupings. I felt for her sports bra and what it had to contend with. It was like herding two open range rabbits into a tiny hutch; that poor bra had absolutely no chance. She did some warm up squats and I watched on in trepidation as the elasticated leggings tried to carry the extreme load. Surely they would fail in their gargantuan task.

But apparently not and five minutes later a suitably lathered up Felicity was ready for her personalised exercise regime and her date with Cathy, queen of the Peleton workout.

As she walked across to the static bike area, I scanned the room looking for nothing in particular. It was a busy late afternoon with so many people trying so very hard to become someone else, someone new, somehow better. Men growing muscles on steroids, using the weights area as an excuse for socialising. Women, hair tied back, fighting their years of excesses, knowing the ultimate solution lay under the surgeon's scalpel. That select body of Knightsbridge and Chelsea special people, all grouped together by privilege and money, all expressing their mutual fears of growing old by engaging in acts of collective masochism.

But those very fears and worries about the quest for eternal youth also made them eminently recognisable for what they were. Wealthy. A breed apart. No room there for the hoi polloi; the monthly subscriptions took care of that.

Which is why I was so struck by the movements of one particular individual. He'd stand out in this crowd all day long. Tall, sinewy, muscular, he was cruising the room, ignorant of the daily melodrama playing out right in front of him. Six two, maybe two hundred and ten pounds of hard muscle covered in tight black tracksuit bottoms and a white vest. All capped off with a deep dark tan, the sort you don't get in the local high street tanning booth. But it wasn't his vaguely porn star appearance that stood him apart. It was his trainers. They too were black, brand new, in fact the only things missing were the price tags. Nothing like the carefully tarnished, delicately scuffed white sports shoes all the locals wore. He looked totally out of place.

But he didn't care. He was prowling, sweeping the gym, looking for something or someone and as I watched in silent fascination, his eyes lit on her.

Felicity was none the wiser of course; she was too busy, head craned back, staring intently at the screen above, gripping her handlebars and pushing down on those resistance pedals as if her whole being depended on it... and it probably did. Cathy the cyber queen didn't care, her financial future depended on Felicity's insecurities, so long may they continue.

Meanwhile the porn star strolled casually across the open space towards her, skipped behind her station and dropped a folded note on her bag as he passed by. Then he was gone. He just stepped out of the room, onto the street and maybe out of my life forever if I didn't get a move on.

I shot down the stairs and caught sight of him loping out of the building, moving easily but with deceptive speed towards Hyde Park corner. I had no time to reach Betty so I set off after him on foot, preying he wasn't going too far. Or too fast.

His was an easy gait as he breezed up Grosvenor Place, me struggling manfully in his wake trying to keep pace one hundred yards behind. Needless to say my Gucci shoes and Versace jeans were highly indignant when faced with their new purpose in life. Not to mention my sheepskin which I ripped open to ventilate my already sweating body as I grunted with the effort of trying to keep up.

He swung around the Intercontinental and up Park Lane, me hoovering any available air about one hundred and fifty yards behind by now. About halfway up Park Lane he was suddenly swallowed up in a doorway and disappeared. I was grateful as I arrived a fashionable thirty seconds later still sucking up the Park Lane exhaust fumes. Stopping across the road from the doorway I looked up at the discreet signage announcing where I was: 'Grosvenor Apartments'. A doorman with green tunic and a suspicious stare was looking right back at me. And I wasn't surprised. I was bent over, hands on knees, fighting for any oxygen, toxic or not. I put my hand up by way of a salute which he completely ignored as he pored over his suspicions about what he was looking at.

I took evasive action and turned into Mount Street, regretting I had ever waved at him in that moment of panic. Too late for that now.

I stumbled into a recessed doorway across and down from the entrance to Grosvenor Apartments. I stayed there for ten or fifteen minutes, enough time for me to regain my composure along with a complete set of fully functioning lungs.

I was just about to leave when the big man reappeared, this time dressed immaculately in a two-piece black suit, white shirt, grey tie and black loafers. His clothes must have been tailored because there were no fabric stretch marks around his outsize arms and legs. His black hair was slicked back and he strode with purpose to the curb where he called a cab and was immediately free and clear.

I, on the other hand, was stuck on the pavement fifty yards away with my metaphorical thumb shoved firmly up my metaphorical arse, wondering how long the walk back to Betty would take.

Some private investigator I'd turned out to be…

Eventually I found my professional pride lying in the gutter on the way back to my car. And it wasn't long before I was sulking in the safety of my dusty little fifth floor office, comforting coffee in hand.

I was still there at six when I called Felicity. I wanted to know what was in the note the porn star in the gym had left her as well as to give her a debriefing on what little I knew of her stalker.

No answer, so I left a message for her to call me, locked the office up and headed home.

CHAPTER TEN

When I drove into my basement car park there was a note taped to the back wall of my reserved spaces.

'IF YOU FEEL LIKE A DRINK WE'RE IN THE PIG'S
-HEATHER'

She was, of course, referring to the Pig's Trotter, a smart trendy cocktail bar just round the corner from my place. It was where all the beautiful people went to socialise with each other and get elegantly caned. I was a regular canee and had an easy relationship with the bar manager. He made a perfectly smooth but secretly lethal Long Island iced tea. So I stepped out into the cold November night air and five minutes later I was easing into the warm seductive atmosphere of the Pig's. The lights were softly dimmed as I walked through the maze of easy armchairs and across the small dance floor to the bar which stretched the full length of the room.

The place was already busy and I couldn't see Heather so I settled on a bar stool and ordered my signature drink.

"How's it going Sam?" asked the barman as he went about fixing my cocktail.

"Not too bad Will, if you like your coffee cold and your women colder."

We both smiled at the simple truth of my words.

Will had been on duty a couple of weeks earlier when my pretty new friend, a woman who I'd known for less than a month, had slapped me across the face and stormed off when she caught me kissing the neck of one of the drinks hostesses. They constantly cruised the floor, taking orders from lonely suckers like me late at night. Clearly not my finest hour and I hadn't seen hide nor hair of the slapper since. But the hostess and me, well that was a whole different story. We'd got to know each other very well, a sort of friends with benefits kind of thing.

He slid my drink in front of me and then moved away to serve someone else, leaving me all alone. But not for long. I felt a slight tap on my shoulder and as I turned on the swivel stool Heather was right there in front of me with only my drink and my stunned silence standing between us.

"Hi there, car wrecker."

Right there and then I thought I'd died and gone to heaven.

It could have been the tight fitting black mini skirt stretched taut over her flat stomach. Or the cream silk, cap sleeved collarless shirt and the ivory silk buttons. Or the silk black Manolo Blahnik 'T' bars with spikes. Or even that diamond and white gold Cartier love bangle hanging carelessly off her right wrist.

But whatever it was I was completely overwhelmed. Talk about punching above my weight? That idiom didn't get near covering the gulf in sex appeal between us. Not even close.

I couldn't look at her without giving myself away, so I just tilted my glass in her general direction and took a huge gulp of that liquid fire. I was trying to damp down the huge emotional storm raging through the very fibre of my being and the drink was meant to help. It didn't.

I managed a fumbled greeting as I turned my bar stool to create the space she needed to fill the one next to me. Our knees were touching and that charged electric current running between us was almost too much to deal with. But it was all I could think about. She repeated her slur on my character.

"How's your day been, my little Mercedes mauler?"

She touched the back of my hand as she spoke and the sudden shock of the contact confused everything so completely that I could hardly remember the question, far less form a coherent response.

"You know in some countries what you're doing right now would constitute sexual assault?"

I looked straight in her clear blue eyes and tried moving my fingertips across the bar to hers. Eventually they touched. She didn't withdraw. And right then I knew I was in real trouble. We were both looking down at our hands, saying nothing, just soaking in the magic of that moment. Or at least I was.

I pulled my hand away in an attempt to claw back control of my dignity and not appear quite so desperate. I took another huge slug of my cocktail and let the music and the atmosphere seep back into our space. But someone had to break the unbearable silence, so eventually I did.

"I met your sister today; thanks for the work. She's not much like you though, is she?" Heather looked up and smiled.

"Well you say that. But beauty is in the eye of the beholder. I'm sure there's someone out there for her. The thing is, she's easily misunderstood. Believe me, behind that delicate nervous exterior there beats the heart of a lion."

Yes... a totally Springbok engorged lion.

I let it go. Slagging her sister off wasn't going to get me into Heather's underwear and that was quickly becoming a matter of some significant importance in my seedy little mind. I needed to change the subject.

"Hungry?"

"Famished, but not just yet. Come meet my friends." She flashed her eyes deep into mine.

And the way she answered made me wonder whether we were still talking about food. I really hope not. But that dark twinkle couldn't be ignored, not by me anyway.

She'd clearly started the night early and was now in that accelerated mood of warmth and comfort that comes more and more naturally as the alcohol courses through the veins.

She was also in a real hurry to introduce me to her pals. So I was unceremoniously dragged off my stool, snatching my drink with me while I was pulled across the room and into a throng of pretty people; young men and women all anxious to live tonight as if it were their last. There was a lot of noise in among the greetings and laughter as Heather described how we came to meet. Then excited partygoers came crashing in all around me, shouting above the music and seeking explanations. I just managed to catch Will's eye for a refill before I went down under the party tsunami...

Three hours later and I resurfaced as a fully paid-up member of Heather's crazy gang. I hadn't paid for a drink all night, that's how impressed everyone was with my treatment of Heather's eighty grand Mercedes convertible. And as the night wore on my tale of daring-do got less and less likely as I drank more and more. By the end of the night the Heather's car was on bricks, the engine having been removed by my criminal vandal friends. I didn't care what I was saying because I'd found new skills as a professional dancer. I never knew I could cut such dashing shapes on the dance floor. Well, everyone else seemed to be laughing at my psychedelic sixties moves anyway.

Heather had left about nine, arms wrapped around a stupidly good looking big bloke who I immediately hated with a passion. The lights were low, but I didn't need to see much to bet he was going to get a lot more than her arms wrapped around him soon.

Oh well, who was I kidding? I had about as much chance of getting close up and personal with her as a one legged man in an arse kicking contest.

Also by that time I'd met the new love of my life, Katey. She seemed hell bent on getting me totalled. And she was doing a good job of it too. It was time to drink away all thoughts of Heather for the night. I had another appointment with a Long Island, and I didn't want to keep it waiting.

I didn't want to keep Katey waiting either.

CHAPTER ELEVEN

I lived in an exclusive serviced apartment block, concierge and all, south facing, spectacular views overlooking the Thames, all the beautiful people hunched up together for comfort.

The watchword there was privacy.

And I owned the penthouse, one of the few remaining benefits from my debauched trading days.

But that wasn't going to help me this morning. In fact nothing was going to help me this morning.

I must have crashed on my sun terrace last night in the cold night air because that's where I was now. Sprawled face down on a sunbed, completely naked apart from one shoe and a sock, with a duvet hanging off me.

I was incapable of any serious attempt at movement so I opened an eye and squinted my resentment at the cold grey morning staring back at me from the balcony. Somehow I got my watch in front of my face. I reckoned I was lucky it was still on my wrist. But it told me I was in trouble.

I needed to be in the office by nine, not slumped on a makeshift bed clutching my balls for warmth and my head for comfort.

I wrapped myself in my bedding, stumbled into the lounge and through to the bathroom. While I converted myself back to a human being in the shower I tried and failed to work out how I'd got home. Not that it mattered that much, I'd come to no harm. And it wasn't like it was the first time either. I was still contemplating the options on what had happened last night when my stupid ring tone shattered the peace and quiet. I found my mobile in the key bowl at the front door along with all my plastic cards and about two hundred quid in scattered notes, most of which had fallen on the floor.

I fished out the phone and Maggie was on the other end.

"Are you coming in today? Only there's someone here to see you and we both know you don't get many visitors."

Very funny.

I told her I was on my way and went back out onto the terrace, cradling only a bath sheet and a black instant coffee which I needed more than life itself.

Half an hour later I was walking through my ante room door, past Maggie's desk and into my office. There was a man sitting in the corner. And not just any man. It was none other than my own porn star postman jogger, yet again miraculously transformed. This time he'd swapped his dubious gym wear for smart blue slacks, coffee coloured soft shoes and a cashmere rollneck sweater. It was slightly stretched against his tight muscular torso. His blue woollen full length coat was draped over his lap, like he wasn't sure how long he'd be there.

If he was expecting to surprise me then he'd succeeded.

I went round my desk, pulled my chair out and sat down opposite him. I looked up. He looked back at me and for all the world I thought he was wincing at my appearance. I shrugged as I spoke as if to try change his mind.

"It's nothing. I do a late night dance set at a local pub."

He obviously didn't get the humour. I ploughed on.

"Well at last we meet. I can't tell you how much damage I did to my wardrobe chasing you around London yesterday."

I smiled what went for a disarming smile without believing I was disarming anyone, least of all him. He spoke for the first time.

"Yes, and I can't tell you how unhappy the doorman Yashid was at having to follow you back to your offices to find out who you were. And on that, why were you following me?"

He didn't seem at all interested in the answer as he walked past me and over to my office window. I stood up and walked over to see what he was looking at. We were both looking at the private preparatory school across the road, or more accurately the school gym situated on the fifth floor.

As we looked on a six-year-old boy sprinted across the gym, past the windows and executed a double pike with twist over the pummel horse.

He only needed one corrective step to steady himself. It was genuinely awesome.

"Wow! Did you see that?" I turned back to my own athletic stalker boy, but he had moved across to the wall displaying my private investigator credentials.

He seemed fascinated by my licence to practice as he answered.

"Yes, my children attend that school; it has a terrific reputation for sporting excellence. So how long have you been doing this sort of work Mr Cove?" He pointed at my licence.

That was the second time I'd been asked that question in twenty-four hours and I still didn't really want to answer it. I was much more interested in how that little boy across the road could have performed such heroics with so little apparent effort. But somehow I didn't think that was what he was in my office to discuss.

"Five years. How long have you been sending threatening notes to young women? And I didn't catch your name."

We were both too close to one another now and a handshake was simply out of the question without stepping back. He didn't seem likely to do that and I wasn't in the mood either. So we just stood there, looking at each other. Finally he turned back to his corner chair and sat down. I did the same. He was still staring at the gym over the way as he tossed his business card across the desk at me. It told me very little apart from his name and contact details. It was time I found out why he was in my office.

"Mr Waldhan, I've been retained by Felicity Scott. She says you're following her and intimidating her with threatening notes at home and elsewhere. Is that right? Are you harassing my client?"

Waldhan looked pained as I described his behaviour, but he didn't interrupt. Finally he spoke in a broken voice.

"That woman's got a hell of a lot to answer for. She's fucked my life, and her brother's fucked my wife."

His head dropped into his hands, and he was looking down at my threadbare carpet when I saw the first tear drop. It disappeared into one of the few remaining threads. His shoulders twitched. We both looked at his single tear for a second, neither of us knowing what to say. This bloke in front of me was definitely not the crying kind. And yet there he was, weeping openly and freely with a complete stranger, wiping his face with the arm of his soft cashmere rollneck as if it were some sort of comfort blanket. Silent protection against any further pain.

"What are you doing here Peter?" He looked up and I could instantly see into his misery.

"How would you feel about a woman who's so evil she's turned my wife against me and ruined my entire business in the process? I hate her. I could kill her."

CHAPTER TWELVE

If there was an *Idiot's Guide to Detective Work* then the first page would be emblazoned with these unforgettable words:

'NEVER TRUST A STRANGER'.

In fact those words would also appear as a footnote on every subsequent page of that very thin book, just as an aide memoire.

Meanwhile I had sucked in every single syllable of Peter Waldhan's sorry tale as if it were all true, which it couldn't possibly be.

According to him, he had met his wife Jenny on the Paris Metro. She was being held at knife point by two swarthy looking immigrant types at the time. But that morning they were incredibly unlucky. Peter was there. And Peter was a karate black belt, sixth Dan. After failing to persuade them of his credentials he had to show them. When he'd done that he threw them onto the platform at the next stop and he and Jenny were off to the best possible start.

When he told me that I gave him another quick once-over and decided he was probably true to his word. It wasn't his chiselled features, or his square jaw line. It was in his eyes. His cold lifeless eyes. They looked straight through me like I wasn't there. He might just as well have had 'DON'T FUCK WITH ME' tattooed on his forehead.

Anyway, twelve months later Peter and Jenny were married at the Chelsea Register Office and settled in the area to raise a family. A couple of years on and they'd started a family.

More recently Felicity had winkled her way into his inner sanctum, his family life. As a fully qualified Montessori nanny, she'd been hired to take care of their two small children. The idea was that Jenny could get out more, meet new people, make new friends. But in fact Jenny and Felicity had quickly become inseparable. According to Peter, Felicity had it in her mind from the outset to compromise his marital arrangements. Felicity had a very active social life and Jenny had been alone a lot. So Jenny was quickly subsumed in the lazy morals of Chelsea's suburban lifestyle, moving easily in and out of Felicity's social orbit. She was introduced to a lot of people, as was Peter, many of whom were only out for a good time.

One of them was Felicity's brother James, who got on famously with Jenny straight away. Peter was suspicious right from the start. Jamie claimed to be an interior designer though Peter had never been shown any of his work. But at the same time Peter was preoccupied building a high profile reputation as a City broker selling bonds and futures for a major bank. So he didn't pay enough attention to Jenny's new found freedoms until much later. Much too late in fact. He only realised he had a problem one night when he walked in on her at their favourite bar. She was having drinks with Jamie. Apparently she had asked for his help with the redesign of the nursery although he didn't look old enough even for designer stubble according to Peter. Peter's anxieties were compounded when Jamie started making regular visits to their house, always on the pretext of selecting wallpapers, colour palettes and children's design themes. At the same time Peter noticed Jenny was becoming more cold, more distant, more easily distracted.

Finally, two weeks ago he'd confronted her after he found a text from Jamie on her phone. The text confirmed a secret rendezvous when Peter was due to be away in Paris on business. They had a blazing row and she eventually confessed. She was in love with Jamie and wanted time to work out her feelings.

Within a week they were discussing divorce. She wanted to take the kids away and start afresh with Jamie. Nothing could be said or done to change her mind. For her it was just a matter of timing.

Things happened quickly after that. Peter immediately fired both Felicity and Jamie. But within days the divorce petition was on his doormat. It landed the same day Jenny threw him out of the family home. He moved into Grosvenor House, using it as a temporary base while he sorted himself out. But he was devastated. He felt betrayed. Mad with anger and jealousy. He was convinced that Felicity and James had planned the whole thing to get their hands on his money. He was particularly incensed by Felicity's duplicitous behaviour.

"If I could have got near her then I wouldn't have been responsible for my actions. I feel the same way now."

It was the chilling way he said it that left no room for doubt; he meant every word.

But his intimidating notes to Felicity had been a mistake. They had only ever been intended as warnings. Peter had threatened to go to the police and have them both charged with embezzlement. But he didn't know whether he would or could ever follow through on any of that. And in fact all he'd done was to give Felicity ammunition to shoot him with, to further damage his reputation in the eyes of his wife.

By now I was looking at Peter in disbelief. Did this sort of thing really happen in leafy suburban Chelsea? Were relationships so fragile? And if it did and they were, then was there any legal recourse? Was it illegal to fall in love with a woman for her money? I didn't think so.

But it was all so grubby. The sort of stuff I usually stayed well clear of.

It was hours later when he finally slunk away from my office, angry and sullen, cursing his hatred for his nemesis Felicity. She had obviously become a bit of an obsession with him; his hatred for her was all consuming.

Unfortunately, he'd left behind him a big decision for me. Did I even want to get involved in such a miserable mess, one where it was too easy to trip over the lies, too improbable to believe the truths you were told?

And did I even care enough?

In any event if Waldhan and his truths were to be believed then all roads led back to duplicitous Felicity and her desperate Machiavellian plotting. She didn't seem quite so innocent any more. I needed to find out. So I called her.

She picked up immediately. I brushed aside her childish apologies for not returning my call earlier and we arranged to meet for coffee at a local bar later that afternoon.

I reminded myself about our last meeting when she seemed so unsure, so troubled, such a victim. She wasn't going to get away with her innocent rambling naivety a second time.

Before I left I called Heather. I was still reeling from our previous night's encounter and I wanted to see her again. Predictably she went to voicemail so I hung up. Maybe she'd call back to see how I was and maybe she wouldn't. Either way I would be learning more about her.

Felicity pitched up at the bar on the dot at four thirty. I'd arrived before her, a habit cultivated during my formative years at public school. It was a simple and efficient way to avoid the cardinal sin of being late and becoming slave fodder, fagging for the animals masquerading as house prefects.

I stood up as she approached looking sure footed. I stayed that way until she sat down, another habit formed at school. This time the discipline had been drilled into me to avoid the cruel words, admonishments and physical punishments meted out for discourteous behaviour. Cruelty delivered without recourse by house masters completely obsessed by their belief in their own omnipotence as professional educators in their own private scholastic fiefdom.

However, it should be said that my contrived manners were normally intended as general act of deference and courtesy, typically extended as an appreciation of the femininity of the opposite sex. Not to this fat arsed hippo coming my way.

She was dressed in what looked like a second hand WAAF two blue piece jacket and skirt. She could have been mistaken for an extra stepping off a World War Two film set. Presumably, she'd given up the option of high street shopping because of the constant disappointment she suffered. Maybe Air Force uniform surplus was her only way forward.

She didn't seem to care at all.

We waited in silence as I ordered coffee for two. Then I leaned forward into her space.

"I spoke at length with Peter Waldhan today. You know Peter, he's your former employer. And it turns out he's the one following you, leaving you notes, trying to frighten you off. But you already knew that Flick, didn't you? You don't mind if I call you Flick? I feel I know you so well now I've spoken to Peter. So Flick, I reckon it's time you explained yourself and your brother James. In particular what have you two have been up to behind Peter's back with his wife?"

I sipped my coffee and waited.

The colour drained from her face, leaving the make up to fend for itself. And it wasn't up to the job. Without a flesh coloured backdrop, the foundation cream suddenly looked far too bright and the mascara had no colour to match up with. So she was in danger of turning into the archetypal circus clown caricature. I smiled involuntarily.

The anger sparked in her eyes.

"What's so funny, Mr Cove?"

Her whole attitude had changed. And she no longer looked in the slightest bit uncomfortable about her situation.

"Yes I knew it was Peter when I asked for your help. So what? I needed to prove to Jenny that he was a complete arse, and you did that for me. So thank you for that. Now I think I'll tell Peter you've been playing fast and loose with his secret little sex buddy, Katey. Yes I saw you two last night in the Pig's. But be careful with Peter. He's devilishly possessive and liable to bouts of extreme jealousy and anger where his women are concerned. Be that as it may, there's nothing he can say that'll get around the fact that his marriage has failed and his wife loves my brother."

Flick had suddenly come alive; she was sat bolt upright now and her nostrils were flaring as she prepared her next assault.

I wondered where yesterday's fragile innocent young woman had gone as she stood up to leave.

"This meeting is over. How much do I owe you?" She produced her wallet to pay me.

She was right, the meeting was definitely over. She paid me in cash, but only after I'd provided a hand written receipt for her services. Then she turned on her heel and left.

I watched her go, amazed at how she managed to get her arse through the double swing doors without using her side profile to squeeze through.

But playing fast and loose with Katey? Peter's secret sex buddy? Like I knew! And jealousy in a martial arts specialist? Not good on any level.

None of that was my style and I didn't like it. Not one jot.

CHAPTER THIRTEEN

Back at my offices I had a message from Heather asking me how I was and requesting a Friday evening repeat performance at the Pig's. She also offered an apology for leaving so abruptly the night before. She'd be there from around six if I wanted to see her.

If I wanted to see her? It was five in the afternoon, just enough time for me to shower and change.

I got to the Pig's fashionably late at six thirty and was greeted by Will's signature drink at my usual bar stool.

Heather was nowhere to be seen and I quickly downed my first Long Island. I was halfway through my second when a few of my new 'pals' turned up for their regular Friday night binge. Still no Heather.

But I was reintroduced to Katey who was no mean substitute. She was one of Flick's many casual acquaintances and, according to Flick, she knew Peter as well. But none of that had anything to do with me. I was just a lonely man looking for warmth and solace on a cold winter's night. Anyway, the previous evening we'd hooked up and were having a great time getting to know each other before she'd left.

We talked trivia for a while and drank together until eventually that warm glow crept over me and the alcohol began its special subversive work. I decided not to mention I knew about Peter and her. I was having a good time and maybe even better times were just ahead. Anyway, Flick's warning about Waldhan must be preying on my mind; I'd even imagined I'd seen him in the bar earlier. Best to forget about him now... That was easy, Katey had my full attention.

She was dressed in a loose fitting white cotton dress cinched at the waist by a figure hugging leather belt with the immortal Chanel interlinking 'C's as a clasp. I wasn't normally a keen fan of brunettes, but with her tightly braided ringlets, her bare shoulders, long tanned legs and her four-inch spikes, she was starting to look very appealing. And the more I drank, the more appealing she looked. She pulled me onto the dance floor around midnight and we moved together, very slow, very close, in sync with the blues jazz which filled the room along with a host of the finest pretty people Chelsea had to offer.

By now I was feeling good about life and even better about Katey as we held each other tight, entwined in that crowded space, bound together as if we were one. I'd had far too much to drink so I didn't care as my hand carelessly slipped down from her waist and touched the top of her smooth taut bottom. She whispered something filthy in my ear as I moved my other hand onto her hip with a featherlight touch. I turned her so that her back was against me and slid that hand across her flat stomach onto her tummy and slightly below. Then slightly lower, then lower still until my hand was almost between her legs and my other one was behind her, feeling the contour of her bottom. I leaned into her neck and kissed her ear lobe as I ran my hand from between her legs, up her front, over her delicate breasts, on to her neck and throat. She was swaying to the rhythm and my hands were back on her hips as I pulled her gently towards me from behind. I kissed the nape of her neck, at the same time running my hands freely over her body. She suddenly swivelled to me and opened her warm mouth on mine. Our tongues touched and we were locked on to one another at last. My hands were all over her now, exploring her whole body through her skimpy dress. There was no bra as I smoothed my hands across her, gently caressing her nipples, our mouths open, hungry for each other. The music had stopped, but we stayed gripped to one another, desperate for the magic of that moment to stay with us, knowing it wasn't possible.

I walked her over to the crowded bar and asked Will for another round, but he was already on it as she turned to face me. We looked at one another but no words were spoken. There was no need. I simply put my arms around her and kissed her hard, with the sort of urgency I hadn't felt for a long time. She immediately responded and I felt her hand easing my trouser fly buttons apart as she felt me through my shorts. I was rock hard as she gently squeezed me but I kept control of myself as my fingers strayed up her dress and down into her wet knickers. She put her head back and caught her breath when I found her dripping moist cunt. I withdrew my fingers and licked them right in front of her.

"That's some taste Katey. Give me more."

As I was speaking, she gripped my fingers and pushed them back between her legs. I could feel all that warmth and wetness smoothing between my fingers as I pressed the heel of my hand against her pubic bone, massaging her at the same time. I didn't want to stop, but people were watching us now; I could feel their envious eyes on us both.

I stepped back, making way for our fresh drinks; Katey looked singularly unimpressed as I swallowed half the contents of my glass in one swig. It was time to make my play.

"What do you want to do now?"

I think I may have had a pleading tone in my voice. But I shouldn't have worried. She finished her whisky sour and then most of the rest of my drink in one.

"The same as you. Come on, let's go. We've got some fucking to do."

I did as I was told. Because she was right.

CHAPTER FOURTEEN

Ten minutes later we were back in my place, I was fixing us drinks on the terrace and we were looking at the London night skyline. I was still coming to terms with what had just been going on only a few minutes earlier.

"Well, that was a first. You must be a convent girl."

Katey smiled a very naughty smile. "And you must be a frustrated public school boy."

Inside the intercom buzzed.

Who the fuck could that be at one o'clock in the morning? I left the balcony to find out. Katey stayed outside, taking in the crisp night air. It was concierge ringing up from reception.

"Good evening Mr Cove, I'm sorry to disturb you at this time but there's a Mr Waldhan to see you. He says it's urgent."

There were two things wrong with that message. Firstly, how did Waldhan have my address? And secondly, what could possibly be so urgent that he needed to see me at this time of night? I supposed I'd better find out.

"Send him up Dougie"

I shrugged my shoulders, apologised to Katey for the intrusion and went back inside to greet Waldhan at my front door.

No one was more surprised than me when as I opened it I walked straight into his swinging right fist. He caught me plum on the bridge of my nose; I heard the crack as the bone moved slightly under the brute power of the blow. So did the glass coffee table, collapsing under my weight as I sailed across the room using it as a landing pad.

Then he was inside the apartment and that whole space suddenly felt very small. I struggled to get up out of the shattered glass but I was too late. He picked me up like a rag doll, ripping my carefully manicured Versace sweater half off my back in the process. Not that it mattered; that jumper was already covered with the blood running freely from my broken nose. Before I could cover myself he hit me again, hard in the mouth. I may have passed out momentarily but I was definitely back in that glass debris, crawling around on my hands and knees, struggling to clear my head. He seemed to like picking me up because he was at it again, this time hurling me back against the lounge wall. I slid slowly down to the floor and when I got there I checked my teeth just in case there were any left. It felt like they were all present and correct, but not for much longer if this mountain gorilla got his Neanderthal way. Now I knew what those two muggers felt like that morning on the Metro. God only knows what I'd look like if he set to work with his martial arts skill set. One thing was for sure; I had to stop getting knocked down and get up off the floor if I was to survive this nightmare.

I wiped my bloody mouth against my sleeve as I pushed off the wall and launched myself at Waldhan with all my remaining strength, just enough to knock us both off our feet. We rolled away from each other but he was up first, balanced on his toes in his karate attack stance. He swivelled on his hips and aimed a roundhead kick as he moved in for the kill. I ducked under it in desperation and planted a left uppercut right under his bollocks. He screamed involuntarily and went down like a sack of shit, clutching the memory of his balls which were now repositioned somewhere near his kidneys. And there was no way I was going to give him time to find them. I stumbled over to him and kicked him in his face. Not much about the Marquis of Queensbury rules there, but I was the one with a battered bloody nose and a massively split fat lip. Unfortunately, it didn't do the trick; all I succeeded in doing was bruising my foot on contact with his hard head. So much for calfskin loafers. He was getting up again and I was in real and present danger if he succeeded. I picked up one of the heavy table lamps nestling in the debris and struck him with it. He grunted and fell back on the floor, giving me desperately needed breathing space.

Why was he here behaving like this? What the fuck had I done to rile him up into this state? I thought now was as good a time as any to ask him.

"Stay down, Peter. What's with you? Seems to me we'd both be in better shape if you told me what the fuck's going on."

He didn't stay down and apart from another grunt as he lifted himself off the floor, he was entirely silent on the matter of my malfeasance. Instead he was shaping to start all over with that karate shit, so I hit him back to the floor again with my trusty swinging lamp base. It was a much heavier blow and this time he stayed down which I liked, a lot. I'd broken my lamp with that last blow. I decided to resort to begging.

"Please, Peter, let's not do this. What's your problem?"

He sat up and leaned against the sofa for support, holding his jaw. Meanwhile I looked around, observing the carnage that was the new hallmark of my luxury penthouse apartment. The large shards of shattered glass scattered everywhere told their own sorry tale. But I was even more impressed by the way Peter had chosen a new blood red colour scheme for my place. Literally blood red. It was all over the deep pile cream carpets and he'd created a completely new visual interpretation of Ralph Lauren's signature wallpaper. The liberal red speckling was now the new feature covering the dark blue/stone stripes... not at all bad. I looked in the wall mirror and tried to guess how many stitches to fix me up, and whether I'd need to get cosmetic surgery on my nose.

Also I wondered how quickly I could get out of this blood soaked clothing and into something more suave, more seductive. After all, I was supposed to be entertaining a guest this evening.

And that reminded me. In all the excitement I'd completely forgotten about Katey. Surely she would find all this excitement hugely sexually arousing. But apparently not. I looked around and she was nowhere to be seen. Maybe she'd had enough thrills for one night.

Peter reminded me he was still around though.

"Jenny left me for the last time tonight. She packed some hand luggage and just walked out with my two little children. And it's all because of you."

Really? Even though I was still groggy I was interested in how he was going to make that claim stick. I shouldn't have worried, he was more than happy to oblige.

"Felicity's just been round telling Jenny about my threatening notes, but this time she had the receipt to prove it, kindly provided by you. And just for good measure she told my wife about Katey and me. What I didn't know until tonight was that Katey had a thing for you too. I think

Felicity really enjoyed that part. She knew it would be news to me, that it would hurt. And she was right. So I went over to the Pig's to find out. And there you were, doing your thing. So where's Katey now?"

He looked around the room and tried get on his feet again. I definitely didn't want that, so I nudged him over on his back with my knee. He looked up, angry and defiant. But he stayed where he was. I was confused.

"Wait a minute. I didn't know you were in a relationship with Katey, and I don't know where she is; I don't even know where she lives. I met her for the first time in a drunken stupor last night. If you've got a problem with any of that then speak to Katey about it. As for Flick telling Jenny about your threats, well it's true isn't it? All I did was my job. What I was paid to do. Now get up and get out."

I lifted him off the floor and shoved him across to my front door. I let him out and closed the door behind him.

That was enough excitement for one night. I went back inside looking for my first aid kit and a big fat glass of Jack Daniel's, purely for medicinal purposes of course.

CHAPTER FIFTEEN

Blood's like unplanned sex. The juices flow naturally in the moment, but next day there's very little trace. Just a few messy memories.

By the time I'd peeled off my various butterfly stitches and straps, apart from some lightweight bruising there was very little to show for the previous late night's gory entertainment.

My lip was slightly swollen, so was my nose, but other than that I brushed up pretty well in the bathroom mirror. Anyway, my dishevelled long hair covered a multitude of sins. The guy looking back at me was in pretty good nick for someone who'd just gone five rounds with a mean jealous drunk who was also a lethal weapon to boot.

Six-foot with mousey blonde hair and still some muscle definition in my thirty-five-year-old frame, even now. I'd never struggled for women and that was my problem. I left school with some good academic qualifications and spent three years at King's College London, learning the tools of the legal trade. But very soon after arriving I realised that a career in the law was not for me. It was so incredibly dull. Three debauched years later, my prestigious degree had got me a position trading futures in the City, a job I was built to do. I was quickly making a lot of money which I immediately swapped for lots of expensive designer drugs to keep me going every day. They say a City trader has ten years to make his money at most, before burn out will finish the job. But if that's true, I have no idea how they hold it all together for that long. For me, the end came after my wife caught me in bed with her best friend, both of us totally creamed on coke and booze. She quit me, and I quit the job that was slowly killing me. It came as something of a shock to find I was slowly running out of money as well and I needed to earn some more. A friend suggested detective work. It was easy he said, there weren't many of them he said and they weren't very good, he said. Being desperate, that sounded good enough to me. I opened up a couple of months later, five years ago now.

But my friend was wrong. It isn't easy because the people you're dealing with usually lie. And everyone thinks they can do the job better than you. And for all I know they probably can. Plus there's a lot of us, all looking for the same easy money, all grubbing around looking for the main chance.

Anyway, reminding myself what a prick I'd been wasn't going to get today's work done now was it?

It was as I was dressing I suddenly realised I didn't have any work anymore.

My only paying client had just paid me off.

I ambled into my lounge and checked my mobile for messages. Heather showed as a missed call last night, but no message.

I shouldn't have worried because I'd just poured my breakfast coffee when the 'phone rang.

"Hello Mr Evasive, where have you been, as if I didn't know? You didn't waste much time last night did you? I was late getting to the Pig's, but when I saw you with Katey I realised I was much too late. So I decided to leave you two lovebirds to it. You looked like you were having a fine old time. Have a good night did you?"

I was delighted Heather had called. I really wanted to talk to this woman about her sister's behaviour, but I wasn't about to do it over the 'phone.

"Are you busy this morning? I'd really like to see you."

She didn't answer immediately and instead kept banging on about Katey and me. But finally she relented, agreeing to see me in an hour at her place which was conveniently situated a couple of floors down from me in the same executive apartment block.

But apart from her sister and our shared building, I was starting to wonder whether we actually had anything else in common at all.

Nevertheless an hour later I was outside 9C, knocking on her door in eager anticipation. It opened and all that excited energy fell away in an instant, replaced immediately with a new dull, gloomy reality. A giant was filling the doorway and all the available space in it. He was much taller and much better looking than me as he pulled the door back to reveal his partially clothed, heavily stacked torso. I was looking at a Greek God, his muscles stretching his skin every time he moved. Worse, his Calvin Klein shorts were all that stood between his modesty and me. And judging by the shape and size of things down there he was packing a lot of modesty.

I recognised him as the same man who'd left the Pig's with Heather wrapped around him a couple of nights before.

I felt the bile and the petty jealousy building in the back of my throat as he gestured me in. The thought of his massive hands pawing over poor defenceless Heather made my stomach turn.

"You must be the oik who's been creeping around digging up the dirt. Come on in grubby arse."

I'd had better greetings, but I wasn't about to argue the point. He walked back into the hallway leading to the lounge and I dutifully followed behind, searching for a smart response but coming up empty.

The hallway opened up into a large corner lounge with two glass external walls running the full length of two sides of the room. One of them incorporated a sliding window patio door which opened onto the outside terrace. The London views were spectacular. So was the body of that gym worshipper who thankfully disappeared out of sight and into another room feeding off from the lounge. I wondered who he was.

"Don't mind him, he's not very good this time in the morning. He can be a little abrupt"

Well that was one opinion. Mine was that he was an obnoxious self-opinionated prick who was most likely ruining my chances with the girl of my dreams.

I turned to face the voice and there she was, my glorious Heather, wearing a short cropped woollen top and jeans but precious little else as far as I could tell. She saw my slightly battered face and stepped back in surprise. She pointed at it and put her hand over her mouth as if to stifle a laugh, though she didn't say a word. Instead we kissed politely. I broke the silence while she went through to the kitchen to make coffee.

"How close are you to your sister?" My words drifted through to the kitchen but there was no response.

"I only ask because she got me beaten up for no reason last night."

There was still no response, no sound apart from the noise of the percolator, percolating. Maybe she was nervously twizzling her pony tail, but I somehow doubted it. I pressed on.

"Did you know she's busy breaking up her employer's marriage at the moment? And her brother James is helping her. Oh yes and I forgot, I believe congratulations are in order; money grabbing Jamie's been so successful he's about to become both a stepfather and a husband all in one movement. So I've got to ask; what the hell is going on?"

Heather reappeared at the doorway with a smile on her face and a tray of coffee in her hands.

"Do you take sugar?" Very cool, very deliberate, very much in control. Very reminiscent of her sister the previous day after she'd paid me off and sent me packing. She sat down opposite me and played mother, just not like any mother I'd ever met or known. Definitely a MILF though. She handed me my mug.

"Well Sam, that's a lot of ground you've covered there. But I think I can help you make sense of it all." She sipped her coffee and continued. "Felicity lives here with me. Jamie too. He's my brother."

She pointed behind her shoulder at the closed bedroom door. Instinctively I relaxed a little as I realised that Heather probably wasn't fucking her own brother. But I didn't interrupt her, she was in full flow now.

"Since Mummy and Daddy's divorce the three of us have become close friends, soulmates even. I know Flick's every move. And Jamie's. I sent her to see you the other day because I reckoned you could help us. Peter Waldhan owes us money and we're going to get it back, one way or another. Even if it means splitting up his marriage. And you did help. Help you've been paid for. So what's the problem?"

She placed her mug on the lounge table as she gestured at my appearance.

"Was that Peter's work?"

She pointed at my bruised face and sat back, crossed her long legs, and let me digest her news. It was going to take a while.

I sat back too and considered what she'd just said.

I'd been played. Right from the outset. And she was in on it. Heather's deliberate parking in my spaces; the subsequent get-to-know-you coffee meeting with her; Flick pretending to be the distressed damsel being stalked. Now Peter was effectively frozen out of his marriage and that was partly due to my interference in his affairs.

What a prick I'd been. Used for Flick's purposes all the way down the line

Katey and I were just collateral damage. Unlucky bystanders sucked in by events beyond our control. An accidental meeting in a bar, booze induced attraction between the two of us, neither knowing of the other's involvement with Peter.

No wonder she'd left my place in such a hurry last night. She must have been scared shitless.

As for me, well I'd served my purpose in this dirty game of kiss and tell for money.

I should go now. And I would, but before I did I felt like clearing that lingering stench in the air. I stood up and went to the window looking down on the street many floors below.

"What an extraordinary woman you are H. A snake, writhing around in your own family pit of vipers. Coiling and twisting, plotting and scheming, waiting for the chance to strike. Peter never stood a chance. Nor did I."

I was staring down at the light traffic below, considering my options.

"Of course you do realise I could go to the police with all this. But I don't know what good it'd do. As far as I know there's no law against falling in love. Nevertheless, Jenny Waldhan has a right to know who she's dealing with here. What you lot are up to. So does Peter. Maybe I'll go have a chat with them."

I turned away from her but Jamie was right there, in my face, blocking my way. So very quiet for a big man. But he suddenly seemed even bigger than I remembered. He was fully clothed now and blotting out most of the rest of the light in the room. Yet when he spoke his voice was soft, quiet, menacing.

"I think you've outstayed your welcome fuckface. Time for you to go."

He grabbed me by the collar, pushing and shoving me over to the front door like his plaything. I didn't much like it, repeatedly brushing his big arms away as he manhandled me across the lounge and over to the exit. But eventually I was outside in the hallway, unceremoniously dumped there, staring back at the door as he slammed it in my face.

I needed to speak to Peter, tell him all about this. I didn't know whether he'd want to speak to me though. I also reminded myself that it was time to get back in the gym. And sharpish if I wasn't going to be pushed around like that again.

CHAPTER SIXTEEN

I went back to my apartment and called him. He needed to know what was going on, what had just been said, who he was dealing with.

"Morning Peter, it's Sam Cove. Don't hang up. I was wondering whether you had time for a coffee this morning. I've just come from the Scotts' apartment and there's something I think you should know. Information I'd like to share with you."

He was surprisingly chirpy this morning. "Yes okay. But this time can we make it somewhere in public, preferably somewhere there's no heavy furniture you can use to beat me with."

Good, he saw the funny side. I'm not so sure I did. After all, I was the one who'd bled all over my apartment. We arranged to meet in the reception area of Grosvenor Suites, his current bolthole.

Yashid was on the door and he looked discreetly away as I stepped through the main entrance. I nodded my recognition and he smiled in acknowledgement. Peter was sat in one of the plush lounge reception chairs by a roaring fire, sipping coffee. We shook hands and eyed each other carefully. I sat down opposite him as he poured me a cup.

"What happened to your face?" He smiled. I didn't.

"Thanks for seeing me at such short notice Peter. I've just come from Felicity's apartment."

I covered the whole sorry tale, leaving nothing out. While I was talking he called the lounge waiter over.

"I'll have a large brandy Michael. Care to join me Sam?"

It wasn't yet midday, but I agreed anyway. I felt I had to wash the bad taste from this morning's encounter with H out of my mouth. I finished my story. There was silence between us until the drinks arrived. Peter swigged his in one and sent Michael away on a repeat mission. I sipped my balloon glass of Remy and let that warm infusion numb my senses as it slid down my throat. Peter looked weary as he attacked his second drink with the same enthusiasm as the first and ushered poor old Michael away under instruction to do the same again.

"You know if you hadn't hit me with that lamp twice, I would have put you away."

That was most likely true, but I had hit him with the lamp base twice and, as a consequence, he hadn't. I reminded him. He let it go.

"So it's a family affair is it Sam? Well that knowledge doesn't change anything now, does it? You see I looked into Jenny's eyes as she talked about that wanker Jamie the other day and she's not going anywhere without him. All I can do now is protect my kids, make sure they're looked after financially. The game's up."

There was a certain finality in those words I didn't fully understand.

But I had to agree. The outlook wasn't promising for anyone unless your surname was Scott. I sunk my drink and ordered another. There was a lot to be said for brunch time drinking. We sat looking into the fire, silently contemplating Peter's fate. Then he looked up.

"I don't know why I got so jealous when I saw you and Katey at the Pig's last night. Even less sure why I followed you home. I don't even care for her much. I suppose I was pissed off with the recent regularity with which other men are taking my women off me. Sorry pal. Well I guess I owe it to myself and Jenny to tell her what she's got into. Don't suppose you'd like to come with me as back up?"

Amazing. Last night we'd been brawling in my lounge. Fast forward twelve hours and we were considering tag teaming his wife. And it made perfect sense too. I should help him. Jenny'd more likely believe me, a private detective, than she would her own husband. And it'd be good to piss Jamie off, even if it was only for a brief while. I agreed, we both finished our drinks and left for his Chelsea home.

I didn't normally do matrimonial disputes, but this one was different. It'd already got me perilously close to a severe beating and even closer to frantic sex… It was becoming personal.

CHAPTER SEVENTEEN

The first thing that struck me about Peter's home was the doorbell. It was a knob handle you pulled away from its hole in the wall.

The second was the sound it made. Like a miniature Big Ben gong going off. And thirdly, I was massively impressed by the size of the guy who answered. My nemesis, Jamie.

Looking his normal massive self, I couldn't work out whether he bought his clothing deliberately three sizes too small, or whether he simply couldn't find a shop where they sold clothes his size. Either way the result was the same; he reminded me of the Hulk, just before he lost it and his clothing started shredding off his body. Jamie was also wearing that 'you wouldn't like me when I'm angry face', not a particularly enticing look. I suppose I should've been grateful he hadn't turned emerald, green the instant he clapped eyes on me.

"Hello again," was my stunning opener. But he didn't appear at all stunned to me.

"What do you two cocksuckers want?" He was on the doorstep blocking the entrance, as usual. But that didn't seem to bother Peter who just pushed past him and on into the house. I, on the other hand, squeezed under his armpit, hugging the doorframe for support as I scrambled after Peter.

"Where is she Tosser?" Peter threw the question back over his shoulder as he marched down the entrance hall and into the kitchen. I assumed he wasn't talking to me. The Tosser in question brushed past me in his efforts to catch Peter up and suddenly we all spilled into the kitchen together. Where all the sharp utensils were. Where I immediately felt distinctly uncomfortable.

And I took precious little comfort seeing the look on Jenny's face when we came in. I'd never met her before but she was one sultry, moody looking woman, with her dark auburn hair hanging loosely over her shoulders, partially covering those deep dark brown eyes. Even though it was still only just after noon she was wearing full make up, with her midnight black lipstick and her slim black manicured fingernails trailing the granite worktop as she came over to be introduced to me. Tosser was instantly on hand to assist.

"This is that private eye prick I told you about. What's your name again gobshite?"

Well that wasn't my name at all, but there didn't seem much sense in correcting him.

"Hello Mrs Waldhan, I'm Sam Cove. I'm here so you can hear straight from the horse's mouth what's been going on. I met him and his sister this morning at their flat."

I gestured dismissively in Jamie's general direction. It didn't have the desired effect. He wasn't dismissed at all. He just stood his ground. Like the granite top he was leaning on, immovable.

"Look Mrs Waldhan. I don't know what your relationship with Jamie is. Or the rest of the Scott family for that matter. But let me tell you about my dealings with them."

For the second time in two hours I repeated my recollection of recent events and that morning's chat with Heather. Jamie fidgeted throughout but made no attempt to intervene. Meanwhile Jenny busied herself wiping down her kitchen work surfaces. It was quite disconcerting watching her ignoring me like that and all done under the watchful eye of Lurch over there, now perched on a barstool far too small for him, just waiting for the moment when he could throw me out of another home…again.

When I finished my rendition she stopped wiping her kitchen surfaces down and paid me some real attention for the first time.

"Mr Cove, why have you come over here just to tell me what I already know? Jamie was there this morning. And he's here now. He's already told me everything. I know all about him and his family."

I sincerely doubted she knew everything she needed to know about Jamie's family, but I reckoned my job was done and that would appear to be that. Suddenly it felt like I should go. And I wasn't the only one thinking that way. Tosser stood up right on cue to do his duty by me. But Peter got up off his breakfast bar stool too, standing in between Jamie and me but all the time staring at Jenny.

"Are you listening to yourself Jenny? Him and his tribe are hellbent on ripping us off and breaking us in two in the process." He pointed at Jamie. "He doesn't love you, can't you see? It's all about the money. And when we're divorced and you've got your half of it, he's going to take it off you, ruining us both in the process. He couldn't care less about you or our kids. I can't allow that to happen."

Jenny looked up at him with a steady stare. Then she walked between us and embraced him. Just a simple gesture of warmth, a recognition of all they'd been through together. Almost as if it were the end of their time as a couple and she were saying goodbye to all their shared history.

She pulled back so she could see him close up.

"Peter, it's all over for us. And it's nothing to do with him or his lot." She was nodding across the room at Jamie.

"It's about you and me. Ever since we moved to Chelsea we've been growing apart. Flick told me about Katey and you yesterday, but I've known something was going on for a while. I didn't need Flick to tell me."

She disengaged and stepped back over to the centre aisle, leaning on it for support. That left the three of us banded together, Peter Jamie and me, looking like the three stooges we truly were.

"I don't blame you; we've just grown stale and dull together. And it's not as if we haven't spoken about it before. But now I'm tired of covering the same old ground. We both know it's over. Let's just accept the fact once and for all. As for your money, I don't want any of it. I never did. And I don't want his family and their outrageous sense of what's right and proper either. All I want is for you to sign the papers so I can divorce you. I know what I'm doing with him. I love him, his lying cheating family and all. In the end it doesn't matter whether it works out with Jamie or not. Either way I'll be free from you."

She waved at Jamie as she spoke. I worried he might start getting a complex if his continued character assassination went on much longer.

And what was that she'd said? She didn't want his money. She really didn't want Peter's money.

There was only one person in the room more surprised at that news than me; and I was looking at him. Jamie had the appearance of the puppy dog who'd just been caught shitting on the kitchen floor. He had moved over to the stool by the doorway, frozen there, a wild look in his eyes, the look of the rabbit caught in the speeding car's headlights with no possible means of escape. And maybe he was getting angry as well. Certainly, he was going green around the gills. I watched on in that moment of pure unadulterated glee as his face flinched in contortion and evident emotional grief, a visible demonstration of his squirming discomfort.

Marvellous. Couldn't have happened to a nicer bloke.

A fly was walking across the quartz worktop and I could hear its footfall in that silent kitchen space. No one said a word. Finally Peter broke the quiet, addressing Jamie directly.

"Did you hear that Tosser? Look at your face! Didn't know about that, did you? Didn't know Jenny was coming to you without the much vaunted dowry? Jenny without a penny. How do you feel now, my outsized parasitic toad?"

Jamie said nothing. He simply unfurled his coat from the back of his stool and left. He had an errand to run, a message to relay to his elders. And his betters.

I looked over at Peter and he was back over with Jenny, cradling the back of her head in his hands, pulling her into his shoulder for safe keeping, just for now. He looked like he was in a lot of pain.

I'd clearly outstayed my welcome so I made my apologies and left to go back to my empty apartment and my even emptier life.

No one was listening, not in that room.

CHAPTER EIGHTEEN

I'd done enough reminiscing for one morning.

That stale coffee smell still permeated my office, Maggie was still sat in reception shuffling papers, memories of Flick's broken body lying flat on the pavement were still etched in my memory. And would be forever.

The late Monday morning local press confirmed Flick's death, describing it as 'accidental'. Maggie rushed into my office armed with the newspaper in one hand and a salmon and cream cheese bagel in the other. I reached out for both instinctively, cramming the food in my mouth, leaving my hands free for the paper. My lips cracked painfully as they stretched tight to accommodate my greed.

The paper confirmed Flick's personal details and proffered a sketchy explanation as to the circumstances surrounding her death. The headline read:

'LOCAL WOMAN DIES IN TRAGIC ACCIDENT'

It went on to state her name, age and address along with the time of death at approximately six that morning. The phrase 'unfortunate accident' was used to describe her dramatic end. The police were keeping an 'open mind' as to the cause of death but were not looking for anyone else in connection with the incident. I pushed my desk chair back, locked my hands behind my head, stared at the ceiling and considered the events of the past forty-eight hours.

Was accidental death the natural outcome given Flick had been in the process of emotionally emasculating then financially castrating Peter Waldhan? It was only three days earlier that he'd wanted to kill her. He'd told me so. He was one man who had every reason to see Flick splashed all over the pavement. And I was personally and painfully familiar with his tendency to violent problem solving.

The press release also failed to cover the inveigling nature of the ongoing family deceit perpetrated by the whole Scott family on the Waldhans.

But what had any of that got anything to do with me? I'd already been used and then discarded like so much unwanted private investigator. My role in this whole charade was over. And I definitely didn't need any more lies and deceit in my life right now.

Nevertheless, I couldn't help feeling the real story wasn't being told.

Not for the first time I felt myself getting drawn into affairs that were best left well alone.

I looked at that wall clock imploring me to get back and involved in another master darts play off. To forget about Flick and her duplicitous family.

I called the Met Police instead.

CHAPTER NINETEEN

DCI Mike Tanner did not look like your common or garden plainclothes detective as he stood in my office doorway that afternoon and introduced himself. It seemed to me he would have looked more at home pitching a tent at Glastonbury, rolling his next joint before the start of the main act at the Pyramid. When he spoke he didn't sound like a policeman either. His smooth public school accent rolled around the room effortlessly, announcing his superiority and class.

But none of that casual intellectual elegance was reflected in his dress sense. His ill-fitting check shirt and faded torn grey jeans did nothing to embellish those loose plastic flip flops covering his slightly dirty grey bare feet. Nor his stringy shoulder length brown hair loosely tied back with an elastic band. But if I was in any doubt as to his origins then his battered backpack hanging in shame from his left shoulder definitely gave the game away. It was Louis Vuitton. Mr Tanner was an aristocrat in tramp's clothing. A complete enigma.

I stared at him in disbelief as he sauntered in and crashed down opposite me in the visitor's chair like he owned the place. I walked over and shook his hand, making a mental note to wash mine as soon as he left.

"Come straight from a stakeout did you Mike?"

He smiled the knowing smile of the man who's faced this type of criticism many times before.

"If you like. So what do you know about Felicity Scott's not so death defying leap this morning Mr Cove? Why did you call us?"

He slipped his rucksack off his shoulder and reached inside for a pen and paper. Old school. Not a laptop in sight. I was warming to him now. And there was another surprise; his Mont Blanc pen was the classic piano black, but this one had what looked like a ruby stone embedded in the clip. Then there was his watch, a Jaeger Le Coultre Reverso in rose gold with a crocodile skin strap. Subtle but impressive signs of good taste in a man dressed like a bag of shit tied up. Hmm... this was one interesting guy. I probed for more information.

"What were you doing when you got the call to come over? And don't tell me you were on royal bodyguard duty because I probably wouldn't believe you."

He smiled again. "Actually I was boarding a plane bound for Thailand, Phuket as it goes."

And I bet he was turning left when he got on the plane.

"So you see Sam, technically you've fucked up my holiday. And all I want to know is, why?"

This man was nothing if not direct. Maggie brought us some percolated coffee and I began my tale of woe. He listened intently, making copious notes all along the way. When I was done he twisted his pen shut, packed it in his bag with the rest of his stuff and stood up as if to leave. But in fact all he wanted to do was stretch his legs.

"Fancy a walk?"

We stepped out of my place and onto the embankment, only a few short steps away. Winter was creeping insidiously over London; the sun had broken through the wispy cloud with that silent hazy way of reminding us of what we were all missing. As we walked we got to know each other a little better. And I liked what I heard. Not what I saw so much, but then you can't have everything in a relationship.

Mr Tanner had been expelled from Eton at eighteen, joined the police and had been with them ever since. Straight out of school and onto the beat. Thirty-five years old, he'd spent the last ten years of his life in CID with the murder squad. So he had real experience of the darker side of human nature. I, on the other hand, came across as a lightweight novice in my line of work, living the life of luxury in my penthouse accommodation deep in the heart of Chelsea. That image was only enhanced by my admission that this was the first time I'd had anything to do with anyone's death, least of all one in suspicious circumstances. My experience was limited to fraud, theft, robbery and the like. I'd always resisted the temptation of the easy money to be made investigating cases involving marriage and infidelity. In doing so, I avoided the pain that was always associated with the breakdown of relationships. And that way I stayed sane. But it also meant I was only ever just one step away from the bailiff's knock on my door.

Mike didn't seem much interested in any of that. However he did seem very interested in the Scott family and their goings on. It was as if he was already aware of them, but if he was he certainly wasn't covering any of that ground with me.

He did ask me one question though.

"If you don't do family infidelities and such like, how come you wound up in the middle of this mess?"

I didn't really have an answer for that one. Except that I had been well and truly kippered by the deliciously deceitful H. And yet what I wanted was to get to know her on a more intimate level if that were still possible. I found it difficult to believe she was tied up in all this. Maybe I just wanted her to be innocent.

But whatever my motives, he didn't need to know about my entirely self-serving nature right now did he?

"Initially I took pity on a woman who seemed vulnerable and afraid. Now she's dead."

We walked and talked for over an hour, but as much as I enjoyed his company, we both had work to do. He had to investigate any suspicious factors surrounding Flick's death. And I had a pressing appointment with a wall clock and a game of spitball darts.

On our way back to my offices he informed me he was going somewhere else so he left me at Sloane Square in a taxi. And that left me alone, dawdling along the King's Road, lamenting the fact that those renowned short skirts the pretty Chelsea girls wore in the summer were totally out of favour in that cold watery winter sunshine.

CHAPTER TWENTY

When I got back there was a voicemail from H. She was almost whispering in cracked and broken tones as she explained herself. It sounded like she'd been crying.

"Hi Sam. Can I talk with you? Flick's dead. I've just got back from identifying her body at the morgue. I don't know what to do right now. Please call me when you get this. I know we didn't part on the best of terms the other morning, but we both know the circumstances were difficult. Now I need some help and I've turned to you. Please call."

Well, my rematch with the long gone and much admired Eric Bristow would just have to wait.

I called H immediately.

"Hello Heather. How're you holding up? I saw Felicity lying on the pavement this morning just after she fell. They were taking her away. It was just awful. I'm so sorry. You must be in a whole world of pain. What can I do to help?"

"Can you come over? Apart from anything else I'd appreciate the company. Especially after the way my brother treated you on Saturday morning."

Ten minutes later I was outside her apartment door again, ringing her bell. Knowing it was entirely inappropriate, nevertheless I thought about what it would be like if I really was ringing her bell, right now. Then I realised if that ever happened in real life I'd almost certainly balls it up. So I shut down that sordid seedy side of my brain as she let me in.

We went through to her lounge, or what was left of it. The police had obviously been at work cordoning off the carnage; their hallmark yellow police crime scene tape was everywhere, stuck to everything. And I was looking at a war zone. The whole place was smashed up. Soft furnishings and furniture were scattered everywhere along with a whole bevy of broken display pottery and other casual lounge art. The coffee table was in pieces and most of the wall paintings had been rearranged, hanging dishevelled on their hooks. The shattered wine glasses were in small pieces all over the carpet, their contents leaving deep red stains everywhere. I was reminded of my own carpet redesign.

Picking my way through the wreckage I found a sofa undisturbed over in the corner. Heather came and sat next to me. It wasn't possible for H to look rough, but she'd obviously been crying because her smeared make up gave it away. I waved my arms around the room.

"What the hell happened here? And where's your gorilla brother?"

I needed to know in case he was hiding in waiting.

"I don't know where Jamie is. But I reckon it's the last we'll see of him for a while, 'til the dust settles anyway. He just packed his things this morning after the fight and walked out. Not even a goodbye."

I was forming a pretty dim view of her brother, but it really didn't matter what I thought about him right now. It only mattered what Mike Tanner thought. I looked down at the remnants of the coffee table top in front of us and there was Mike's card resting quietly amidst the teak rubble. So he'd already been here and taken statements before he came to see me. And he'd forgotten to mention it.

"What happened here Heather?"

Tears fell freely from her eyes as she answered, in fact she was only just about holding it together.

"I don't know. There was some sort of commotion going on early this morning. The shouting and screaming woke me up. But it was the silence after the noise that got me out of bed in a hurry. I came in here and it was like this, with my stuff all over the place. Jamie was on the balcony, scared stiff. I joined him out there, calling for Flick. He looked down at the pavement below, pointing. It was only then I realised the horrible truth. He rushed back inside and started packing and within minutes he was gone. Never said a word even though I was begging him to stay."

She pointed at Tanner's card.

"The police reckon Jamie's got some serious questions to answer. They're looking for him as we speak. I don't know why he ran away. He's done nothing wrong."

I wasn't convinced. Fleeing the scene of what might be a capital crime was illegal all day long in my world. I didn't tell H about my meeting with Mike. I didn't see what she'd gain from that knowledge.

"Well it doesn't look very good for the ape, now does it. He's run away. And the police won't like that at all."

I looked into her azure blue eyes, as clear as the sky on a cloudless day. They were filling up again so I gave her my handkerchief. I didn't think she'd use it. It was Turnbull and Asser's very finest silk in pure blue, a perfect match for her eyes. But I was wrong. She promptly blew her nose in it and held it tight against her chest, ready for another go if necessary. I mean, really?

Terrific. Suddenly I felt like crying with her.

"If he had nothing to do with the fall, then why has he disappeared? Mike Tanner will want to find your brother and quickly. Any idea where he might have gone?"

The tears were running down her face, a silent expression of all her fears and anxieties. And my pure silk, wholly innocent handkerchief was immediately put to the test again. I just hoped it was up to the challenge. Privately I determined to burn it later, innocent or not. She spoke through it.

"I thought he might have gone over to Mum's, or even Dad's at a pinch. But when I called them neither of them has seen nor heard from him in ages. I also tried Jenny but he wasn't there either. That was a bit awkward because I had to tell her why I was looking for him, and I couldn't do that without making her aware of Flick's death. It didn't go very well I'm afraid. But he's been nowhere near her since Saturday. The truth is he could be anywhere right now. And I'm clueless. It's probably best left to the police to track him down."

Yes, but what would they do when they found him? At best he was witness to Flick's last waking moments. At worst... well it didn't even bear thinking about.

I needed a drink so I offered H one and fixed mine at the same time. Those gin and tonics were almost medicinal in their restorative characteristics. After my third I moved to be closer, wrapping my arm around her for comfort and solace. She didn't seem to mind. And I certainly didn't. In fact I was enjoying the intimacy. But I realised none of it was going anywhere. Even in this more relaxed moral state I knew it was time to leave. There was a time and a place for making a move, and this was neither the time nor the place. I left and retired to my penthouse at the top of the stairs, wishing I wasn't such a gentleman and also knowing that wasn't true.

Jack Daniel's wholeheartedly agreed. He knew me too well.

CHAPTER TWENTY ONE

Next morning I got to the office only to find I wasn't the only one there. Mike Tanner was propping up the wall. I wouldn't have recognised him if it wasn't for his distinctive long hair. For a start he was in a crisp white double cuff shirt with onyx links. More impressive was his midnight blue wool suit, obviously tailormade by the way it was shaped to his body.

None of that mattered though because I couldn't help noticing he looked anxious, distracted, tense.

I invited him in, like it was my choice whether he came in or not and poured two cups of my disgusting three day old coffee. I thought that might settle him and it did, but not for long. He was too agitated, pacing up and down, wearing out yet more of the remaining threads in my office carpet.

"We found Jamie Scott in Dover, trying to put himself and his Mercedes on a ferry to Calais. I interviewed him late yesterday afternoon. He doesn't like you much does he? He reckons you're trouble."

I couldn't argue with that, and I didn't.

That's where Tanner had to rush off to yesterday afternoon then. And he must have known where he was going when he was with me.

Nice of him not to mention it.

"Anyway, he was very helpful as it goes. And it's all so simple as it turns out. In fact it couldn't be simpler. Apparently Felicity fell over the balcony by accident. They were having a row about Jenny Waldhan and Jamie's intentions towards her. Things got out of hand and Felicity threatened to cut him up into small pieces with a kitchen carving knife. Seems it's quite normal to resort to GBH in the Scott household if the girls aren't getting their way."

His matter of fact manner was quite disconcerting; like everything Jamie had told him was irrefutable truth.

But on that basis I made a mental note to keep H out of my kitchen if she ever came near my place.

"It seems things went from bad to worse and Felicity went crazy, chasing round the lounge after him, trying to slice and dice him. Finally in desperation he ran out onto the balcony to escape. He tried to close the terrace door behind himself but she was too quick, she got through the gap and launched herself at him with a full frontal assault. He just managed to duck out of the way in time, her momentum carried her over the balcony and she plunged one hundred feet to her death below. Just like that. A tragic accident brought about by a family row gone horribly wrong. I don't know why I was ever worried about the circumstances of her death now I've got Jamie's take on events."

Mike stopped pacing and threw himself in my visitor's chair. It was groaning all over again.

"I'll tell you what though. He looked like he'd had the shit kicked out of him. Mind you, Felicity was no lightweight was she? He showed me a gash on his forearm where she'd managed to catch him with the blade. So there it is, an open and shut case."

And then he sat bolt upright.

"But d'you know what? I didn't appreciate Felicity was that athletic, that nimble. She must have been to leap ten feet over the terrace furniture to get at him, miss and go clean over the balcony. And Jamie must be one of those pretend gym buddies; to look at his ripped physique you'd think he'd easily be able to evade his sister's loving embrace or fight her off even. At least you'd have thought he might have got away if he'd tried hard enough. And he doesn't strike me as the shy retiring type. Presumably, he hadn't tried hard enough then."

It was my turn to think.

"Have you questioned Heather? She was in the apartment when it all happened. She might know more than she's telling."

I knew he had; I'd seen his calling card. And when he looked at me he knew I knew he had. But he still raised an eyebrow and looked askance at me, like I was a runaway from the funny farm or something.

"Of course I've questioned her. She maintains she was in the bedroom and saw nothing. When she came out it was all over and Jamie was alone on the balcony, frozen with fear."

I looked across slightly surprised.

"It's a very convenient tidy explanation of events isn't it Mike? You think that's all there is to it?"

He got up and started pacing again.

"It doesn't matter two fucks what I think. It's what I can prove that matters. And at the moment all the evidence points to accidental death."

He looked genuinely perplexed, upset that all he had was Heather's and Jamie's word for what had happened. Then he came over all inspirational on me.

"So I was thinking. You've got some sort of relationship with Heather haven't you?"

Well I thought maybe I did, but you never could tell. I'd got pretty tipsy with her the night before and left her place thinking I might be in with a chance. But who knew? What was on Mike's mind? It didn't take long to find out.

"Why don't you succumb to your more base instincts and get closer to her? The closer the better. You never know, she might open up to you. Because yesterday I listened to the biggest load of bollocks for what happened on that balcony that I've ever heard."

With that he turned to leave. I tried to stop him, to get him to expand on his suggestion that I spend more time with Heather, gaining her trust. In much the same way I attempted to engage him on the matter of my fees. I tried to introduce him to the idea that I had a living to make and he was asking me to use my time to help him out.

He leaned against the doorframe, impatient to go yet hearing me out anyway. But his silence on my proposed remuneration package told me all I needed to know about my chances of getting any money out of this.

He left and what remained with me for the rest of the day were a whole load of thoughts I would be better off not having. Thoughts about the flimsy nature of Jamie's explanation; thoughts about what might really have happened the previous evening.

I phoned Peter Waldhan to bring him up to speed with Jamie's movements. He suggested we meet around ten the next morning at his Chelsea pad for a communal catch up.

CHAPTER TWENTY TWO

Ten o'clock the next morning and I was on the steps of Waldhan's house. I wasn't really looking forward to the next hour, but Jenny had a right to know her future wasn't as quite as bright as it had once looked. For a start, the love of her life might very well be prime suspect in a murder case. So she might be looking for a new lover as well as a new nanny.

I pulled the bell handle and Big Ben rang out for the whole street to hear. Peter answered and showed me through to the kitchen. Jenny was there, just as before. Looking totally at ease with herself and her circumstances, just as before.

I talked them through the police involvement and their current lines of enquiry. Most importantly I covered off the fact that Jamie had been caught at Dover and had given some bullshit version of events about Flick's death.

Jenny didn't look quite so easy in her surroundings anymore. She clutched the back of her breakfast bar stool for support.

"You two are lying. You're both lying."

She was pointing at Peter and me. And she looked pretty pissed off with us both.

"You're just trying to pit me against him. You're working together. Where's Jamie now?"

She was pleading. For her he was an innocent abroad in need of succour and solace right now. To me he was a prime suspect with an uncorroborated story that simply didn't ring true. I didn't know his whereabouts and I told her so. I suggested she contact Mike Tanner at the Met. Nevertheless it was a good question. Where was Jamie?

As I left the house the Waldhans were busy recreating their life history again, reminding each other where it had all gone wrong. Very loudly. With lots of expletives.

I just hoped the kids weren't home.

CHAPTER TWENTY THREE

Back at the office my thoughts turned to the lying, deceitful, manipulative, cold, sensitive, sexy, irresistible Heather. And what she knew.

Maybe she was having the same thoughts about me, because later that afternoon she called and invited me out for dinner. I should have refused on principle, but that was never going to happen. She asked if I liked Indian food and I told her not to be stupid. She was attending an early evening cocktail party in Bruton Street so we agreed to meet outside Benares at eight.

I didn't much care for W1 generally or Mayfair in particular. The residents had an inflated opinion of their own importance and it showed both in their ostentatious properties and their deeply self-serving lifestyles. So I didn't get up to Mayfair much socially. I preferred the more relaxed atmosphere of Chelsea because the people there were more at ease with themselves.

That was when they weren't lying and cheating to one another behind closed doors.

As if by way of retribution for my renegade thoughts, the heavens opened just as I stepped out of my taxi in Berkeley Square bang on eight o'clock. I wondered whether it might be a premonition. The rain was torrential outside Benares as I waited for H, then waited some more, slowly drowning in the deluge. I hadn't thought to bring an umbrella, but luckily I was wearing my painfully expensive YSL full length suede trench coat. I was definitely dressed to impress. And that would have been fine if it hadn't been for the advice I'd been given by the sales assistant when I bought the coat: 'Don't wear it out in the rain, you'll ruin it.'

So in the end I'd bought a coat that wasn't fit for purpose. Even though I'd been warned. But no. Instead I'd paid for the high end fashion look without any functional attributes and now that decision was back to bite me hard in the arse.

By the time she rounded the corner by Jack Barclay's showrooms I was completely sodden, my coat stuck to my body in desperation. Meanwhile Heather was dry as a bone, fully protected by her Mercedes golf umbrella. It must have come with her car. I should have stolen it when I dumped my rubbish in that Mercedes a few nights ago.

We kissed politely before going in; for my part it was a bedraggled wet excuse for a kiss.

Inside, the cloakroom attendant stripped off my suede homage to fashion as half its full length slapped on the marble hall tiles under the weight of the water it had absorbed. There was already a small puddle developing on the floor below and he held it away from him like it might be infectious, carrying it at arm's length to the relative safety of the cloakroom. Meanwhile H just clicked her golf umbrella release button while another attendant shook it clear of raindrops and took it away. As we stood in that reception facing one another, the differences between us tonight were laid bare for the whole world to see. Her pink Dior knee length two piece was underscored by a simple white cotton blouse that barely showed under the ruffles of her wrist cuffs. Below the knee her pink Pigalle Louboutin court shoes revealed those delicately muscled calves in all their tanned glory. Critically she was entirely unaffected by the savage conditions outside. I, on the other hand, looked like the Creature from the Black Lagoon. Pissed wet through, rat tailed hair sticking to my face and neck, two tone Alexander McQueen double cuff black and white striped shirt looking distinctly one tone, stuck to my body in desperation. Even my Ralf Lauren trousers were clinging to my thighs for grim death, all of me dripping steadily and unremittingly onto the welcoming carpet just inside the restaurant entrance.

I must have looked absolutely yummy.

I put my arms out in despair, looked her straight in the face and laughed at the miserable wet rag of a man I undoubtedly was. She joined in the joke that was my appearance as that poor attendant returned with a thick towel. To my horror he began dabbing me down in his half-hearted effort to dry me off. A lesser man would have cried. But not me. I emerged embattled but undefeated, with my new Worzel Gummidge hairstyle and the sodden memory of my once pristine clothing hugging me in its wet embrace.

We adjourned to our table and ten minutes later the food was ordered, drinks were in hand and all was forgiven, though never to be forgotten.

I'd booked a booth away from the main restaurant light, tucked away in a corner, just as planned. The Montrachet was cold and crisp as the golden liquid slid out of the crystal glass and onto my palate. But it was as nothing looking into her crystal clear blue eyes with the warm table candlelight flickering in them. Her face was candlelit too, those flickers dancing across her cheeks and down her soft delicate neck. Our hands were far too near to one another; I so wanted to feel that electricity we had shared that first evening at the Pig's. And it was close. Our knees were touching again and my emotions were toast. But Mike Tanner's words sat with me; perhaps I might get more out of her than he could. The small talk dwindled as I ordered our second bottle of the golden nectar and smiled across at H.

"It's really good to see you tonight, so soon after the horrible events of yesterday."

She looked down at her wine and slid her hand over the back of mine. When she looked up her eyes were soft with tears.

"We posted Flick's death on Instagram last night. Just a wreath and a requiem. The response was heart breaking. She really was loved by everyone."

Now while I didn't know Instagram from instant coffee, I did recognise the language of death. I placed my other hand on hers. A tear dripped on it then rolled off and onto the white table linen. We both watched, fascinated at its progress to the end of its journey. To be honest I had no words for her right now and I'm not sure she was looking for any. Finally I raised my glass and spoke.

"Here's to Felicity and the new challenges she faces. May God's grace go with her."

It wasn't much, but it was all I had.

I decided Mike Tanner's plans for us would have to wait.

The rest of the evening was a relatively subdued affair. The food was exceptional, the wine so delightful that we drank far too much of it and the company was warm and affectionate. Talk of what had happened in her apartment the previous morning seemed somehow redundant right now. Anyway, I was too busy drowning in the pools of her eyes. There was something about this woman.

Three hours later and the moment I'd been dreading all night was on us. The taxi ride was over and we were outside her front door, no more than twelve inches separating us, as we had been all night. She was looking for her keys and it might well be that the magic of the evening was nearly over. I was desperate to hold her, kiss her, embrace her. But the timing wasn't right, not tonight. I stepped back and kept on moving away. I wished her a good night with sweet dreams as I turned, scuttling along to the lift then pressing the 'UP' button repeatedly. I don't know why I bothered. She didn't come running like in the films.

Back down the corridor I heard the quiet click of her door closing behind her.

CHAPTER TWENTY FOUR

The previous evening in a failing attempt to appear relaxed and nonchalant, I'd suggested a friendly breakfast at Joe & The Juice on the King's Road. So next morning I was back in the bathroom, preparing myself and wondering why I was so clumsy around Heather. I didn't have many friends, but none of those I had would ever call me nervous or shy around women. And my record stood as testimony to the fact that they liked me right back. But there was something about her that set me on edge, made me unsure of myself, stirred up all my insecurities. The man looking back at me in the full-length wall mirror was pretty well defined, muscular, with deep penetrating green eyes and a mischievous twinkle in them, or so he'd been told. Something was going wrong for that man then. I was nervous at the very thought of seeing her again even though it was only eight hours since we'd said goodnight at her door.

Still, as I smoothed on my Dior Bleu, me and the bloke in the mirror could both agree that today was another day, another chance to shine. I squeezed into my Boss chinos and slid my Versace grey cashmere shoulder button jumper over my torso. I slipped into my grey Gucci suede loafers for good measure. Grabbing my hip length Billionaire sheepskin, I swung out of my glorious penthouse and into the bracing November morning. I felt a billion dollars as well. But in fact I was just hoping there were enough visible signs of opulence and wealth covering me to give camouflage and some flimsy protection from her piercing gaze.

I seriously doubted it though.

She was already seated and tucking into her Serrano sandwich when I arrived. When she stood to kiss me she smelled divine. Almost edible. I sat down and ordered a power shake and spicy tuna wrap, praying she didn't ask me what was in the power shake. Thankfully, she didn't.

"Thanks for last night Sam. It was good to get out and forget about things for a brief while. But today it all begins again. I've got to meet the funeral director and arrange the funeral, all that depressing stuff that'll just bring up all the old memories."

I'd found myself a straw so I clutched at it.

"Need company?"

As I spoke, a shadow appeared in the doorway and the room was suddenly slightly darker, even though it was nine in the morning. Jamie hove into view and slumped in the sofa chair opposite me.

"Hi H. Hello dickhead. Not spoiling anything am I? Reporting for duty as requested."

He saluted H and sneered at me.

His constant insults were beginning to wear thin. I took comfort in the fact that he looked like he'd done five rounds with Anthony Joshua. The beating he'd taken from Flick had definitely left its marks. His face was still puffy and swollen.

H looked over at me with a sympathetic pout and replied.

"No, I'm good thanks Sam. Jamie's coming with me for moral support."

Well good for Jamie. It seemed to me he'd be better served cruising the streets of Chelsea seeking out his next mark now Jenny was a no go. I decided to push back a little.

"So Jamie, how'd you get on with Mike Tanner? He tells me you were chased around the room by a knife wielding crazy woman. Must have been real frightening if you ended up on the balcony with that nasty little cut on your arm?"

The sarcasm wasn't wasted on him and he rounded on me. He suddenly looked angry and dangerous.

"I wasn't afraid of her, Dick Prick. I was afraid for her. I let her hit me, cut me. She wasn't thinking straight. We tried to calm her down but she was having none of it. Everything happened so quickly I had no time to stop her going over."

He stood up, towering over me.

"Anyway fuckwit, what's it got to do with you?"

Fuckwit stood up to face him.

Heather was up on her feet too, forcing herself between us.

"Now children, play nicely."

She turned me away gently pushing me back down into my seat. Jamie was still standing way too close to me, but eventually he sat back down too.

There was an uncomfortable silence while we each digested what had just happened. I decided Jamie didn't much like having me around and worse it was making H feel uncomfortable. I made my excuses, waved H politely goodbye, collected my spicy tuna and power shake from the counter and left, exercising as much dignity as I could muster.

But back at my office I replayed what Jamie had said. He'd used the word 'we' when he was describing the attempt to calm Flick down. But I was under the impression he was alone with Flick throughout the incident. Heather had told me so. She'd said the same to Mike Tanner. So had Jamie.

So either H was lying and was in the room when it happened, or someone else was in the apartment early that morning. Another witness.

Either way it presented me with a major dilemma. My professional credentials were now on the line. Mike Tanner needed to know about this. But in telling him I was also putting H in harm's way.

Fortunately, the phone rang and interrupted those dark thoughts. It was Jenny Waldhan.

"Mr Cove, can you come over and see me? I want to talk about Jamie."

CHAPTER TWENTY FIVE

Betty pulled up outside the Waldhan residence an hour later, scraping the kerbstone with her rusty old running boards as she did so.

I had no idea what Jenny wanted. Last time we met she had accused me of trying to destroy her future with the new love of her life.

The bells chimed and she was framed in the doorway, looking fresh, renewed.

"Come in Sam."

We went inside. I was shown to her sun lounge out back, beyond the kitchen and halfway to Surrey, or so it seemed to me. When I eventually got there I was in a conservatory, early winter sun streaming in from above, fragrant flowers discreetly placed all around. I sat in a lounger as big as Betty while she stepped over to the Nespresso and created a coffee for us both.

"I saw Jamie again after we spoke on Saturday. And funnily enough he was having second thoughts about our relationship, now there is no money. He felt it was getting too messy, he sensed real antagonism from Peter and in any case he had to give his time over to the family arrangements following Felicity's tragic death. In short, he dumped me. You were right. He's a complete cunt."

The fact that I had never used that word to describe him was irrelevant. That word should never leave a beautiful pair of full-blooded lips like that. I was shocked and it must have shown.

"Yes, I'm angry Sam. I gave him everything of myself, including my marriage. And as soon as I sought to seal the deal between us he ran away because he can't afford my lifestyle. I asked you here because I wanted to apologise for my behaviour. But I also want your help. Paid help. I've done wrong by Peter, I know that. And I want him back, I know that too now. But I've got a problem. She's called Katey Wilson. And he's been seeing her for a little while, all through our difficulties. I'm worried it might be more than a fling. Peter told me about your disagreement over her. So I want you to finish what you started and take her away from him."

It didn't happen much to me, but I was genuinely speechless as she reached for her pocket book and wrote out a cheque. She walked over and handed me the signed note. I looked at it. Ten thousand pounds.

"That's for taking the job; there's another ten when that bitch is out of my life."

I thought I heard the noise as my chin hit the highly polished marble conservatory floor. I knew it was only a matter of time, but eventually I had become a sex worker. I put my square designer cup down in its square designer saucer and looked her straight in her sultry eyes.

"Look Jenny. I know you've been through a lot recently. And I know you've been hurt. But hiring me to sweep up the sexual debris doesn't sound like much of a plan. I have no hold on Katey or Peter. I have no idea about the strength of their relationship. Christ, I didn't even know Katey's last name until just now. Two strangers looking for company, that's all we were. We met twice in a bar and that's it."

"Sam. This isn't about her. And it isn't about you. It's about saving my marriage. I've made a terrible mistake. Now it's all about my two children and their futures. And it's about my need to get my husband back. Will you help me or not?"

Right then there were at least two conflicting thoughts racing through my addled brain. And that space was so small they didn't take long to make the trip. First, she deserved another chance at her marriage given the way it'd been hijacked by the Scotts. Second, I wasn't much for getting involved in other people's matrimonial troubles. It only ever ended in pain and misery. Usually mine.

But there was a third, lame, ignoble thought dragging behind the other two. And I was familiar with it; I'd had it many times before. I had no work and none on the horizon either. But right here in my sticky little fingers was a way to change all of that in a moment. And maybe do a little good at the same time.

That tired old thought won through. As always.

"Okay Jenny, I'll do it, but Peter's got to agree to it as well. I don't fancy another three rounds with him if I can avoid it."

She called him and he agreed instantly. I knew he would. He'd already told me about his feelings for Katey the other lunchtime at the Suites. She had been an emotional crutch for him during his time of difficulty and nothing else.

He said he was agreeing to my involvement for the sake of his marriage, but I wondered whether it was more for the sake of his bank balance.

In any event I had the green light to find out how durable Katey's feelings for Peter really were. And given what had already happened between us I was pretty sure I knew the answer.

CHAPTER TWENTY SIX

I left Jenny to ponder her future and after a long walk through her house I eventually found the front door.

Surprisingly, Betty was still where I'd left her, right outside, running board resting provocatively on the kerb stone trying to attract attention. But no one had thought to steal away my prize possession. I looked over at my little green piece of a brighter yesterday as I skipped down the doorsteps and out onto the street. Betty was a one off, a thing of true beauty. One bump over the right front wing from a reversing scaffolder's flat back which had misjudged its parking distance five years ago. Thankfully, the bright orange indicator had avoided the carnage. The scraped front boot from when her brakes failed at the traffic lights last year and I drove her right under the back end of a bus. You could still see the red paint on her bodywork, but no harm to her front boot love handle, thankfully. As I slid inside and onto her cracked leather seats, her minimalist dashboard with protruding wires was a gentle reminder of why she remained at large on the streets of London, and not stolen for resale in the Middle East.

I called Mike Tanner. Scotland Yard wasn't too far away and if Betty could make the trip I could be with him in ten minutes. I had information about Flick's death. He invited me over immediately.

The policeman guarding the entrance smiled discreetly as I pulled up and explained my presence. A quick call elsewhere, the barrier was up and I was parking below the Metropolitan Police building with instructions on where to go when I got out of the lift. Mike was there to meet me at the lift doors on the third floor.

I don't know what I was expecting when I entered his office, but it certainly wasn't this. The sun was streaming in through a wall of glass overlooking the Thames. Mike had prime views of the river traffic and all the imposing architecture along the embankment. We were so close to the river launches it felt like if you reached out you could almost touch them.

So that's what my taxes were being spent on. I'd often wondered.

It was a huge office space, with one relaxed seating area facing the view and another more formal interview space over in the far corner. I sat down in the Conran retro style minimalist sofa as he handed me my coffee and I contemplated the piss poor nature of my comparative existence.

"So what do you think, big boy? Just like your offices eh?" Mike was sitting opposite me, smiling his disarming smile and I was being totally disarmed. In fact if I'd been gay I'd have launched myself across the coffee table at him in a heartbeat. He looked so clean living. Healthy. Crisp blue shirt with dark grey trousers hanging insolently over his highly polished military style shoes. He looked every inch the high ranking officer in the Met Police that he so obviously was. And absolutely nothing like that swamp rat I'd first met back at my dreary offices.

All apart from those free flowing locks. And even they were a reflection of him as an individual in a modern day, fully socially integrated police force. What an advert for twenty first century policing he was.

But I didn't think he meant that when he asked me what I thought about his office.

"It's a bit on the shabby side don't you think? And all that glass. Those windows must be a bugger to keep clean."

As I spoke, outside those windows a twelve-foot cradle dropped down right into my eyeline and the two harnessed window cleaners went about their work. One of them even gave us a cheeky wave. Like the plonker I was I waved back, smiling, slightly embarrassed that I'd even done it. Mike took the cue, laughing as he waved with me.

"So what is it you've got to report young Sam?"

I told him about my dinner with Heather, about the social media tributes to Flick. I also mentioned being hired to get Jenny and Peter back together again. But somehow I forgot to tell him about my breakfast at Joe's, or the fact that there might be another witness to Flick's fall. I needed to check out Heather's involvement in any of that first. I knew I didn't have long to do it either.

"So what you planning next for Heather? When are you seeing her again?"

I explained that she was busy today, but I'd be seeing her later in the week. He had more news though.

"By the way, I've got a tail on Jamie, but don't let that bother you. If you bump into him just act naturally. And try not to get in a fight like this morning! How was your spicy tuna by the way?"

Jamie's tail was very good.

Suddenly I realised I needed to take care with this man. He probably knew quite a bit more than he was letting on. I wondered whether he knew about Jamie's slip of the tongue too.

We said goodbye and I went back to Betty and the Darts Challenge Cup. He went back to work in his luxurious office suite with London's premier view of the Thames.

CHAPTER TWENTY SEVEN

I got Katey's number from Peter and called her later that afternoon. I hadn't seen or spoken to her since that fateful evening at my place and things might have been awkward. But in fact she was deeply apologetic about running out on me in my hour of need. So I milked it for a while, but soon we got past that. I asked if she was free that evening and she was. And I knew she would be, given what had happened on that dance floor at the Pig's. She was well up for my suggestion of a sleazy night's jazz over at the Dover Street Club. We set the time for nine. She seemed very keen. So was I.

Predictably I got there early and checked in my coat, leaving a message at reception for her to join me downstairs when she arrived.

I never got tired of the Dover Street Club. It was moody, dark and above all, full of action if you were looking for it. Running alongside the small intimate dance floor on one side was the band rig, on the other side, the bar. At the far end, stepped back from the people traffic, was the secluded dining area. Its intimate, dimly lit tables for two were crammed so tight up against one another you could hardly squeeze into the chairs, but as a consequence so close you could talk over the live music. And while the food would never be Michelin standard, it was certainly edible and after all, the main item on the menu was jazz.

I stepped down from the street and into the basement gloom, my eyes adjusting to the new ambience as I went. The room was already crowded even though it was mid-week and I still had to jostle for position at the bar. Five minutes later and the Long Island was slipping down, easing me into the night ahead. I was midway through my third drink when she arrived and I didn't see her at first, I was too busy acquainting myself with my latest cocktail distraction. But when I looked up I didn't know how I could have missed her. As she descended the stairs people were moving aside to get a better look. She saw me and waved. Three hundred heads followed her wave across the room, their gazes all settling on me. The disappointment on those faces was palpable when they realised what they were looking at. To be fair I knew what they meant. I was no rock star, no film god, no high flying politician. I was just an ordinary bloke who had got incredibly lucky.

But they were right; I was definitely punching.

As she walked towards me I filled the time by admiring her turnout and finishing my drink in one. Everyone else in the room was still staring at us. And I wasn't yet in such a state that I was either steady or ready enough to deal with what was walking towards me.

She was dressed in a blood red figure hugging dress. It was split up to mid-thigh and it must have been sprayed on. Every contour of her toned body was on show as she eased across the dance floor like she was parading on a catwalk. A catwalk built just for her. No VPL, no underwear. No possibility. Just the red gladiator four-inch spikes with ties that wrapped half way up her tanned calves. And an excuse for a matching red handbag with frayed red ties. It was only just big enough to hold my one travelling condom.

If I'd ever ask her to carry a condom for me.

If I even had one.

If I'd ever even had one.

If I'd ever even known how to use one for that matter.

She walked straight up to me at the bar and slid right into my space, standing ridiculously close. Everyone got back to the serious business of drinking and pretending they were happy. She whispered in my ear.

"What's a girl got to do to get a drink in here?" She kissed me lightly on the cheek and I was suddenly so hard I had to turn away in case it bumped into her hip.

I ordered her a whisky sour as a tribute to our last evening together. I got myself yet another Long Island because I was going to need it. I also called in a couple of tequila shots as back up to get the night rolling. I was going to need them too. Finally I turned back to her armed with the shots and a supporting act of salt and lemon. We clinked glasses and drained them, immediately licking the salt from the back of our hands then rushing to the quartered lemons for sharp juice relief. Anything to disguise that disgusting burning taste. About as enjoyable as walking across a white hot fire pit, but pretty cool as an ice breaker. We laughed as we felt the aftertaste of that nightmare ritual, but thankfully the cocktails were on the bar to comfort us. I glugged half mine and tilted the rest towards her.

"You could have made some sort of effort if you knew you were coming out to play." I gestured at her outrageously promiscuous dress code.

"Are we playing games tonight then, Sam? Is that what we're doing?"

She cocked her eyebrow as she sipped her drink and looked quizzically over the sugared rim at me.

She was far too close and I was definitely erect and standing to attention as she pressed her hips up square against me. She smiled as she answered her own question.

"Oh, I think we are." She moved her hips against mine, in sync with the club dance music playing. She swallowed her drink, cupping her hands under my glass as an invitation to follow suit. As I did she slid her hand into mine, slowly easing me onto the dance floor behind her.

It was rammed with clubbers, party people all geared up for the live music now only a few minutes away. I was geared up too, holding her hand tight in case I lost her in the crowd and never saw her again. She took me into the middle of the floor where there was no space, nowhere to move, nowhere to hide. She pulled me to her, sliding her long slim arms around my neck as she did. I moved toward her as if in a trance, wrapping myself around her, pulling her very close. I could smell her scented hair, brushed her neck with my lips, moved my hands slowly, softly, up and down her back. And all the time we were gently swaying to the mellow tones of Aretha feeling like a natural woman. Just like I was feeling this incredibly naturally attractive woman tight in my arms. We didn't speak. There was no need. The music and the mood said it all. But finally the spell was broken as the jazz band introduced themselves to loud, raucous applause. Grudgingly I disengaged and led the way to our pre booked dinner table over in the shadows, holding Katey's submissive hand behind me as I led the way over to our table.

I pulled her chair back for her as far as I could and we sat down. A waiter appeared out of the morass, wondering about the wine. We hadn't even looked at the menu yet, far less the wine list, but I sent him away to find a bottle of chilled Mersault and some Perrier. I settled back to look at Katey properly for the first time.

And what a stunningly beautiful woman she was. Back at the Pig's I'd been hammered so I hadn't really paid too much attention to her finer features. Or any of her features at all actually. All that had mattered then was that she was presentable, able bodied and breathing. But looking at her tonight was like looking at her for the first time. Now I was able to take in her truly striking beauty. Deep auburn ringlets, dark green eyes and a smooth complexion with only a touch of makeup. Rich full red lips with a pout to make you melt; a long, elegant neck I'd already gently kissed; petite breasts demanding a soft sensual caress; and her firmly muscled bottom perched exquisitely on top of those long silky legs. A bottom just aching to be touched, squeezed, massaged. And this woman that every man in the room had noticed and wanted was sat almost in my lap, looking for any signs that I might want her too. Unfortunately, I was still semi sober... and fully intimidated.

I didn't speak for a while, I couldn't. Any conversation that came to mind sounded laboured and clumsy in my head. Thankfully, the loud insistent music came to my aid for a while. But soon the silence was getting awkward. I felt like asking her stuff like where she lived, how she knew Peter, what she'd had for breakfast, in fact anything to fill this massive and echoing silence between us. But it was far too late for those niceties. I picked up my menu like a cardboard comfort blanket and noticed she'd done the same. Great stuff Sam. I was clearly boring her shitless. But still no chat from the Chatmaster though. It was as if I was frozen in time. I looked around for help and signalled the barman for more cocktails. A couple of minutes later he obliged and finally I was safe behind my refill.

Katey on the other hand had clearly decided to put me out of my misery and take matters into her own hands. It was the only thing to do given I was behaving like the spotty little oik in the corner of the school disco, praying for the lights to come on and the evening to end.

She leaned over.

"See anything you fancy?" she asked. I looked up from my drink and she was very close, whispering. I took another drink before I replied.

"I'm looking at it."

I moved across the few remaining inches between us and then we were kissing. Soft, sensuous, lingering kisses that took no account of time or space. She dropped her hand off the table and placed it just above my knee as our tongues touched and our kisses became more and more urgent, more demanding. Her hand travelled on up my thigh and then there it was, feeling me, hard, through my trousers.

The ice was well and truly broken now.

We were still kissing, exploring each other with our tongues as I reached across the table to hold her. Suddenly there was a loud cough next to me. I looked up and there he was. The very uncomfortable wine waiter. Cradling the Mersault, the sparkling water and the accompanying ice bucket, all balanced on a silver platter. He looked slightly uneasy, but not nearly so much as us. We decoupled and sat back to create serving space at the table for him. He was avoiding all eye contact as he went about his affairs. But I caught Katey's eye and she covered her face with her napkin to muffle her laughter. I joined her and almost immediately we were in convulsions. Thankfully, the waiter saw the funny side and smiled as he left the table; his awkward moment was over.

"What is wrong with you Katey? Have you no shame woman?"

She laughed. "I'll show you what no shame looks like later if you're interested."

At that moment, the band finished their introductions and an old black guy with a trumpet stood up to play *Blue in Green*. A Miles Davis classic. The lights dimmed and suddenly all was well with the world.

The food came. It was incredibly average and also very late. But we didn't care. The wine was excellent, the music first class and the company exquisite.

I found it very difficult to concentrate on her chat because I was constantly reminded of her basic, raw sexuality. I noticed she had a habit of drawing her fingers tantalisingly across her lips while listening to me spouting off about some absolute bollocks or other. Or stroking my free arm when I occasionally stopped whittling on and took another slurp of that rich creamy yellow nectar. Or running her foot slowly up my leg as I was sat back enjoying the band paying their continuing homage to Miles Davis. At one point she shuffled her seat nearer to mine during a sax solo and nuzzled the crook of my neck with her forehead. I pulled her slightly away from me and kissed her softly on her lips. I put my arm around her chair and then on to her bare shoulder.

The soloist was quietly, sensuously teasing the soothing love tones out of his sax while the audience looked on, silent in awe and admiration at his talent. We were all transfixed by his skill and passion for his art, etched across his pained face as his instrument cried out the torture of unrequited love. His writhing torment was painfully transparent as he arched his back and looked to the sky, squeezing the pain and agony out from his saxophone, then recoiling and bending over cradling his instrument, nurturing the sweet sounds and passion he was creating.

I could smell her perfume, feel the softness of her hair touching my face. I was already intoxicated by too much delicious wine and the mood music sweeping the room. Her long slim legs were crossed and I put my hand on her thigh, just below the hem of her dress. I was suddenly quite nervous, anxious at the prospect of rejection. But there was no obvious resistance. Her skin was warm and soft as silk. I kissed her earlobe and buoyed by her apparent acquiescence to my hand being where it was, I smoothed it a fraction higher leaving that finger just under the hem. Then I moved it almost imperceptibly a little further. Still no resistance. My finger was still waiting, hiding under that hem, hovering, anticipating the moment when it ran out of leg. Or was unceremoniously removed from the field of play. I thought I felt my heart beating in my mouth. She changed position and turned slightly towards me, uncrossing her legs at the same time. And at that moment something happened. Something had changed.

The saxophonist was still saxophoning, the waiters were still milling around, waiting, people were still crowding each other at the bar area eager for their next drink. The low murmuring hum of the whispering audience was still the same. But in my very small table space there was only the heavy weight of unfulfilled sexual tension, unimageable and irresistible. I couldn't hear or see anyone else. Everything was very quiet where we were. I was falling into Katey's dark green eyes, lost for words, letting the musician's charms wash over our table, holding us effortlessly under his magical spell. My hand inched further up her leg and I imagined her legs moving slightly apart, making way for me. Her inner thigh was warm and smooth, gossamer soft. And I hadn't imagined it;

she spread her thighs open a little more, kissing me, lightly brushing my lips with her tongue as she did. The room was packed to the rafters as was the restaurant space. There were people all around, close up and tight together just a few feet away on the dance floor. The soloist had given way to his band accompaniment and the audience were moving around again, showing their gratitude with massive applause and shouting their appreciation of what they'd been privileged to hear.

But down in the dugout, under the table, other things were happening. I was on fire. So was Katey.

I flipped the linen tablecloth over her lap to conceal my finger tenderly teasing its way to the top of her legs, finally resting on her most intimate parts. Of course there was nothing in the way. How could there be in that dress? She was wet through and I found her warm soft sensitive spot immediately. She groaned and her head went back as I moved my finger gently across her clitoris, smoothing it, touching and moving my finger on her slippiness, teasing her soft, sensitive wet cunt lips as I went. I leaned across, holding her to me as she slid slightly down the seat and held my face to hers, her lips to mine. I was rock hard and feeling slightly lightheaded at what was going on with us, all in full view of the crowd, if they were at all interested. And I was hoping they weren't. But it was she who pulled away first, a fire deep in her eyes as she spoke.

"We should leave."

A simple statement of indisputable fact. I nodded stupidly and threw some cash on the table as I stood up, draining my drink as she grabbed my hand and headed toward the exit with me in tow. I exchanged my coat ticket with the receptionist, barely grabbing my coat off her on my way up the stairs. We fell out of the club and into the fresh cold night air, bundling past the queue waiting to get in. She pushed me up against the wall outside, devouring me with her mouth, her hands all over me at the same time. The urgency of her passion was plain for everyone to see. I was aware of some cheering and laughter at my plight as I wriggled clear, wrapping my arm around her as we both jumped into a stand by black cab idling at the kerb.

"Where to guv?" asked the innocent cabbie. I just had time to mumble my address before I was consumed under Katey's body. She launched herself at me, cornering me against the cab door, leaving me nowhere to go but into her welcoming arms.

That cab journey was special. She was all over me, frantic to get at me and my manhood. By the time we got to Hyde Park Corner she was on her knees between my legs unzipping me, one hand squeezing my fuck-ready cock, the other cradling my jewels very tenderly. She kissed the base of me and ran her tongue all along me until she reached my tip. Then she put her whole wet mouth over me and caressed me, wrapping her tongue round me slowly, gently sucking me softly as she did. It was heaven. I genuinely thought I was going to lose it there and then in the back of the cab. But by Sloane Square I had her on her back, my hands all over her breasts and in her cunt, sliding two fingers in and around her as my kisses became ever more brutal, more unforgiving. We didn't know the cab had stopped outside my place until the smiling cabbie gleefully informed us. We got out sheepishly and I tipped him twenty quid on top of his fare by way of a thank you for letting us use his facilities. He chuckled as he drove off and we joined in too, laughing all the way into reception past a sleepy but welcoming Dougie and on up to my starlit penthouse, home of my dreams and excited anticipation.

We crashed through the front door together, both revelling in the knowledge of what was to come. I pulled her across the lounge and pushed through the bedroom door and onto my bed. I was out of my clothes in a few seconds, almost tripping while peeling off my trouser legs in all the excitement. But when I disentangled and looked up she was naked and spread eagled on the bed, wearing nothing but those gladiator heels and a dark moody stare, ready for battle.

I knelt over her, pressing my mouth against hers, drawing my tongue down to her erect nipples, kissing one and gently stroking the other with my free hand. I moved my body down hers making sure that before I did my cock pressed against her thighs so she knew what was coming her way. She arched her back as I rubbed my head between her thighs and finally found my own piece of warm wet heaven with my tongue. It found her quickly, easily as she started writhing, grinding, pressing her pubic bone into my face, grabbing handfuls of my hair, pulling me so close up to her we were fused as one. I let her move to her own natural orgasmic rhythm as she pushed and pulled my head to give my tongue full access to her body. A few seconds later she was tightening up in an emotional frenzy and so was I; we could both feel she was losing control. She moaned softly and caressed the back of my head as her clitoris went dry. She threw her head back, crying out in the pure ecstasy of that moment, a massive release of pent up frustration as her knees locked and her arms froze behind my head while she came in my face. And she kept on groaning as the massive emotional waves crashed over her, again and again.

Finally she was spent. I wiped my mouth on her stomach as I made my way back up her body, leaving my tongue trail behind as I mounted her for the first time. She was pleading for me to fuck her as I put my cock against her dripping cunt and looked deep into her eyes. She was gagging for it, so much so she couldn't speak anymore. For a moment we stayed like that, but I couldn't wait a moment longer so I sank myself deep inside her, right up to my hilt, and again. Then I stopped. My cock was paused, half in half out, seeking her final permission to take what was mine. She wrapped her arms tightly around me by way of her answer, opening her legs wider as I slid my manhood slowly back down and into her incredibly warm wet body. I grabbed her arms and put them over her head as my knees sought more purchase, forcing me even further into her. I was kissing her passionately on her mouth and her tongue was in mine as we moved together, lost in a frenzied perfect harmony. Far too soon I felt myself coming, but she was with me and as I gave way to my desires she was wide eyed herself, coming again as I emptied my very being into her beautiful, soft yielding, young soul.

We came together four times that night, each time a little more understanding, a little less frenetic than the last. But always incredibly powerful.

When daybreak came, so did we, for the last time. Both of us finished husks of our former selves.

CHAPTER TWENTY EIGHT

The morning came and there was a note next to me when I woke up.

'I've got to go; people to see and all that stuff. Given the choice I'd stay in your arms all day long. Last night was fantastic. If you want a repeat performance you only need to call and I'll come running.

Katey

xx.

P.S. It's raining outside so I've stolen your coat from last night… If you want it back come and get it.'

That 'coat' as she so quaintly put it, was a Paul Smith exclusive, a limited edition that had cost me a small fortune in a charity auction. Still she was worth it, but only just.

I fell out of bed and into the shower I most definitely needed after last night's action. As the warm water rolled over me I thought about Katey and what had happened in Dover Street and after.

Before we'd started anything she had wanted me to know about her relationship with Peter. It was as if she needed to get it off her chest, to clear the air.

They'd been seeing each other for several weeks after a chance meeting at the Pig's. Interestingly, it was at a private party organised by Felicity. Things had moved quickly between them and very soon she thought he might be falling in love with her. She knew about his marital problems. She also knew who was causing them. Flick had made no bones about the fact that her brother was madly in love with Peter's wife and that seemed to incense Peter. His loathing for Felicity knew no bounds, which was awkward because Flick was a good friend to Katey and she didn't want to lose her. But there was no doubt things were warming up between Peter and Katey until I pitched up. I offered Katey a simpler, less complicated proposition so she was with me to find out where it might go between the two of us.

On the other hand I had no such long term relationship motives. All I knew was that was some woman I had molested last night; she had no inhibitions and had given me all she had sexually. It was simply the best sex I could remember and there was more to come if I wanted. And I definitely did want.

I decided to report back to the Waldhans. That was the easiest money I'd ever made. Katey was most definitely not invested in Peter at all; last night removed all doubt, unequivocally.

Taking their money for proving it made me feel a bit too uncomfortable though. I felt a bit of a fraud so I had decided to come clean and tell them this one was on me.

I was in my office by nine and the Waldhans' by ten to see them both. I sketched the outline of events the previous evening over coffee in the conservatory. I left out the details about our all night sexploits. Instead I told them what they wanted to hear; Katey had already moved on and was openly looking for a new relationship when the right man came along. I didn't mention it was most likely me. I didn't see the point. Peter had already expressed his feelings on that matter in my apartment a few nights earlier.

But was it my fertile imagination, or did Peter appear a little crestfallen at the news of our sociable evening together? Or the news that Katey was back on the market?

Jenny on the other hand seemed positively elated at the news, turning to hug her husband on the sofa. His response was more perfunctory than enthusiastic.

"So about this fee" I said, hoping to deflect attention from Peter's morose mood. "In all conscience it's too much for what I've done. In fact it was my pleasure, and I'd do it all again for free. It's nice to see you two weathering this storm. And I'm no marriage counsellor, but you do look very comfortable together."

Jenny smiled, acknowledging my attempts at amateur psychology, while Peter stared out of the window at the rain trickling down the panes outside.

However Jenny was having none of my childish interpretation of events.

"Keep the money Sam. You've been worth every penny since you became involved. And here's the balance." Peter absently nodded his assent, preoccupied with his own thoughts. I shut up as I looked down and saw the cheque for the second ten grand payment.

There's an old adage I'd been introduced to at an early age. It was that when you've got the order, get out of the shop. And I'd taken it to heart a long time ago.

So I simply took the payment, said my goodbyes, wished them both well and left them to contemplate their own uncertain future. Meanwhile I wallowed in my own thoughts of how I was going to spend my new found wealth.

CHAPTER TWENTY NINE

There was still a problem that needed dealing with. And his name was Jamie.

The other morning he had let slip that someone else was in the family apartment when Flick fell over that ninth storey balcony to her death. And that person must have witnessed what happened immediately before the fall.

But that wasn't the issue. The real problem was that I hadn't told Mike Tanner about it. And that was because I didn't want to shine an uncomfortable light on Heather's recollection of events that fateful morning. She'd said they were on their own so I wasn't sure why I hadn't told Mike she'd misled us. Maybe I was trying to protect Heather from his intense scrutiny if he found out she'd lied. Maybe I wanted her to tell me first about what had really happened. Maybe I just wanted to give her a chance to retell her version of events without any pressure. Who knew? But what I did know was that when he found out and he would find out sooner or later, he was going to have a view on my silence on the matter.

I needed to speak to Heather.

I got her on her mobile later that afternoon.

"What you doing later?"

"I'm supposed to be over at the Pig's, sort of a wake with the others you know, celebrating Flick's life and all that. But to tell you the truth I'm not sure I'm up to it. Why do you ask?"

I wanted to tell her that her cover had been blown by her brother's clumsy stupidity but I decided to wait.

"Well we had such a pleasant evening the other night I thought we might do it again. Pig's is good for me."

"Okay. You might be right at that. I'll see you there at eight."

I didn't know how the night would go, but I was about to find out.

I walked in and it was Thursday evening so the pretty people were all out to play as usual. I found my spot at the bar easily enough and Will was there a minute later with my drink in hand.

"Who's the lucky girl tonight then Sam?" He placed his hands on the bar and smiled wryly.

"Strictly business tonight my friend, strictly business." I smiled back.

I wondered whether that was true or whether Heather and I might find time for each other as well.

I'd soon know because in walked H, coat casually flung over her shoulder, tight jeans hugging her waist and bottom. She came up to the bar and plonked herself down next to me, dropping her coat on the floor and under our seats for safety. She ordered her Manhattan, turning my way.

"Hello gorgeous, getting needy for me are you?"

She reached for my hand and held it gently in hers. This was going to be even more difficult than I had imagined.

I took a drink and looked up at her.

"Hello H. I wouldn't say needy. But you are guilty of the unconscious seduction of my soul. And I was hoping we might explore that possibility. What do you think?"

She picked up my hand and kissed the back of it.

"I think I'd like that."

I pulled her stool closer to mine so she was right in my space, me in hers. I kissed her softly on the lips. She kissed me back. She wasn't interested in her friends, all of them gathered on the other side of the room drowning their sorrows at Flick's death. Not at all.

Two hours later and the only thing different was the bar tab. I simply couldn't deal with this woman. She had me emotionally cornered, trapped in her beguiling stare, her sensuous touch, her simple but expressive gestures to highlight her feelings. We talked about her and me and then me and her. It was as if there was no one else in our world. My sexual energy was totally out of control; it was a constant struggle to keep my hands off her, but my thoughts were nowhere near as constrained. Nor was my constant involuntary erection. It was so exhausting, all of it. I just hoped she didn't notice my excitement as it constantly pressed uncomfortably up under my zip.

We'd retired to a quiet corner of the club where the music wasn't so insistent and we could hear each other speak.

Finally, bolstered by several cocktails, I was emboldened enough to raise the subject of that mysterious other visitor to her flat. Even though there were many more pleasurable things to do. I took a deep breath and broached the issue.

"Jamie let slip yesterday that there was someone else in the apartment when Flick fell. Either that, or he was referring to you. In any case I think it's time you came clean with what really happened that morning. Because I have a professional duty to tell Mike Tanner what I know; what Jamie said."

I shut up and waited. She looked away, across the room, over the heads of the throng of party people stuck in the frivolity of Flick's parting wake. It was a distant, faraway look, completely disconnected from our current reality. Eventually she turned back to me with a cold glint in her eye.

"I have no idea what you're talking about." She paused to sip her drink. She continued. "I was in bed asleep until the screams and the noise woke me up. When I raced through Flick was gone and Jamie was alone. And that's it. I don't want to talk about this anymore, it's too painful."

She stood up with the rest of her drink, poured it down her throat and walked away across the room to her friends. No goodbye, no looking back, nothing. Just the empty space next to me where she'd been sitting.

I sat there on my own, letting the cool alcohol numb my senses until the glass was empty and I had a big decision to make. Did I get yet another, or did I head off home, a beaten man? The answer was in Will's hands as I walked back to the bar and his welcoming grimace.

"Not so good this time Sam?"

He might have been enjoying my discomfort, but man code meant he'd stay quiet. I saw Heather out of the corner of my eye, sitting, very subdued, over in a corner surrounded by her grieving soulmates.

"I pushed it too far this time I'm afraid. Never mind, one day I'll get that flight path approach run right. Instead of constantly crashing and burning."

He smiled and turned away, leaving me to my own private thoughts and recriminations.

I had no idea what I was going to do now. H had decided to tough it out, deny what had happened at Joe's, even challenge my version of events if necessary. Though she must know it would collapse any hope of a meaningful relationship between us.

But after this evening I knew a lot more about her. Unfortunately, she knew a lot more about me too.

Anyway, I knew I couldn't stay in the bar while she was there so I took that thought home with me as I dragged my sorry arse back to my apartment and called it a day.

CHAPTER THIRTY

I got hold of Mike Tanner first thing the next morning. I had no choice; I couldn't cover for H any more. Whatever she and Jamie were up to, I didn't want any part of it.

He said he'd stop by at the office on his way into work and in exchange I gave him the promise of a coffee he'd never forget. Maggie was true to my word, the rich dark Aribica waiting in the percolator when he walked in casting its own aromatic spell over the room. He threw himself down in the visitor's chair.

"So what's to report Sam?"

He was so very relaxed and at home wherever he was, good looking, clean shaven and apparently unattached. Or so he said. And even though he never mentioned it I was guessing he didn't struggle much for female attention. I answered his question.

"Heather knows more than she's telling you."

I told him about Jamie's slip of the tongue the previous morning. He nodded in recognition of what it meant.

"So she's lied?"

I nodded my agreement.

"Well in that case we need to get her in for questioning don't we?"

I nodded again, knowing that would be the end of any hope for me and Heather.

"And why didn't you tell me this yesterday when you called round to the Yard?"

He looked suspicious and vaguely threatening. I ignored the look.

"Because I thought I could find out. Maybe there was a simple innocent explanation she was afraid to tell you lot."

He looked doubtfully at me but let it go. He stood up.

"Okay Sam, well thanks for that. I'll keep you posted as to developments. Listen, I'm going to be over your way tonight; bit of a retirement bash for a colleague. We'll be at the Blue Bird. I'll buy you a drink if you're there."

I said I'd try and we said our goodbyes. As he stepped out of my office Maggie stepped in all wide eyed and excited.

"Who's that sex on a stick?" she asked as she cleared the cups away.

"I don't know Maggie, I really don't. I thought I did. But now it's definitely worth me finding out."

My next call was to Katey. I wanted to know if she was free that evening but she wasn't picking up. I left her a message that I wanted my coat back.

I was in the Blue Bird alone at eight thirty having decided to take Mike up on his offer. He was obviously keeping things from me and I figured if we struck up some kind of relationship it could only help me in the long run. Also I was interested in the outcome of his interviews with H and Jamie. But mostly it was because I was lonely with nowhere to go on a Friday night.

As I stepped out of the lift on the first floor I could see him and his party in the cocktail bar area, laughing and joking, shouting and bawling at each other like it was their last night on earth and they'd decided to depart this mortal coil on a special high. The place was full, but they had commandeered the dance floor and set up camp at a couple of the sofa suites that surrounded it.

I didn't announce myself, I just moved to one side to watch Mike in action. Dressed in collarless white seersucker shirt and tight jeans, he was centre stage and loving every minute. His flowing locks were quite the crowd pleaser as girls gyrated on the floor, brushing his hair with theirs as they wriggled and gyrated around him, all seeking his attention. He was doing a lot of laughing; well who wouldn't when you were getting that sort of adoration just for being yourself? Other blokes were trying to infiltrate his group of female admirers, but with little or no effect. It was as if he'd cast a spell on that part of the dance floor. He was having his own private party inside a private party. And the champagne was flowing freely. Waiters armed with bottles of Cristal were coming and going at random. There must have been twenty people in the party and somewhere amongst them was the poor retiree police officer. But he was getting precious little attention as far as I could tell, so presumably he was drowning his tears in booze as the rest joined in. Even though the music was revivalist, reminiscent of the eighties disco sound, nevertheless everyone was having a great time bouncing along to it.

And as I looked on I suddenly felt very alone. Maybe that's why I was drinking so much lately. I ordered another Long Island and went back to my spy station to drink and observe.

I'm not the jealous type, but it really was pretty depressing stuff; Mike wasn't even trying.

I must have been there half an hour, getting more bitter and twisted about his nonchalant ease in the presence of beautiful women he hardly knew. And as time passed by a pattern was emerging. Though the room was pretty crowded, most of the best looking women in the place were eventually gravitating his way. They came and they went, the faces changed, but the size of his entourage didn't seem to diminish much. Laughing, shrieking, all seemingly competing for the same man. And he was loving it.

After another drink, then yet another, it was becoming quite irritating to watch. One girl in particular stood out among that bevy of beauties. A stunning woman who simply wouldn't leave him alone. She was hanging off him, stroking his long hair, smoothing the back of his head and nuzzling his neck while he held court, anything to be near him. I wasn't too familiar with the feeling, but early onset envy was sweeping over me in waves. She was great looking, short black hair shaped close to her face with rich ruby lips. Her ample breasts were hidden under her pastel yellow rollneck cashmere sweater, her long brown bare legs teasing out from under a mid-thigh length suede skirt, with brown suede Louboutin heels to match. Truly unforgettable.

One more drink and I was ready to enter the fray. She had become irresistible to me. Unfortunately as I made my move I tripped over a random table leg, stumbling into the middle of the throng, bumping into and nearly falling over her in my anxiety to introduce myself. As it was my drink went all over her arm instead. I collected myself, brushed myself down and carried on regardless.

"Hey good looking. I'm Sam."

I already had her undivided attention; she was busy wiping my Long Island off her and grimacing at me like she'd stepped in a turd. Even through that open hostility I couldn't help but notice her complexion. It was completely clear, unsullied by makeup, shiny like porcelain. And I had a great opener that'd crack that face wide open.

"Can I ask you a question?"

She looked bemused.

"Do you know the difference between a Ferrari and a hard on?"

I paused for effect. No answer, just an empty silence.

"I don't have a Ferrari."

And there it was; my coup de grace, my one liner to end all one liners. Renowned for its ability to kill off any sexual advance stone dead. Delivered right in her left ear.

I didn't know why this particular suicide mission had taken my fancy. Obviously, I was very drunk and I think I was feeling sorry for myself, spiteful of Mike's natural feminine charms. In any case it had entirely the opposite effect to the one intended.

"You fuckin' soak. Why don't you get out of my face?" And with that she punched me in the throat. I was instantly down on my knees, choking, fighting for air through my newly rearranged windpipe. Of course the crowd thought it was hilarious, going wild at my evident discomfort. It was left to Mike to help me off my knees and back on my feet, then to reintroduce me to the assembled masses. I don't know which hurt more, her brutal unsolicited attack, or the laughter of her police mates. Either way I was in no shape to argue the toss as Mike sat me down in a nearby armchair and got me a glass of champagne. I was very quiet, largely because I'd temporarily lost the power of speech. So I sipped my drink and looked disconsolately around the room for any impartial support. There was none. Eventually the raven haired temptress came over, perched in the chair next to mine and introduced herself as Annie.

"Sorry about that Sam, but you really need to work on your introductions. What are you doing here?"

"D'you know what Annie? That's a really good question. I have absolutely no idea. He invited me over but forgot to mention why."

I gestured at Mike who was busy playing with the tie ups of one of his groupie's halter neck tops, totally oblivious of everything else around him.

"Ah, Mike. Yes, he's a very persuasive man."

She was looking at him dreamily as she said it and I could only guess at the history between them.

"So how do you know him?"

I was genuinely interested in what it was about this man that was so appealing to women.

"I'm his sister."

I must have looked shocked, probably because I was. By the way she'd been behaving that was the last thing I expected.

"But you seem so very close."

"We've been through a lot together, that's all."

I had no idea what that meant but it seemed to me that I shouldn't keep prying so I went back to my champagne, sipping it until she broke the silence by asking me to dance.

I fell out of the Blue Bird about three hours later, completely whacked and totally at ease with the world. I had hardly spoken to Mike at all, but that didn't matter because I'd spent the whole night with his sister and I'd left with her number.

There was life in the old dog yet. I must have got lucky.

Then I remembered my last moments with H and my mood darkened, again.

CHAPTER THIRTY ONE

I didn't get much sleep that night. Too many ugly thoughts washed up on my shore, sweeping in on the tide of my emotions. Too many memories of the good times I'd shared with my ex-wife. Matched only by the bad times associated with my infidelity. These late night thoughts were happening more and more lately. I found myself wondering what she was doing nowadays. Whether she ever thought about me? And if she did, what were her memories?

I lay on my back watching the clock slowly ticking down my life, mocking my pathetic attempts at creating something more meaningful, something more permanent than my grisly, lonely, daily grind.

And then demons came flooding in, those faceless terrors; fears of financial failure; ugly feelings and overworked self-criticism; reflections of conversations that could have and should have gone differently; anxieties about deeds done or not done; and worst of all that creeping feeling of self-loathing that eventually permeated my every thought, every waking moment of the early hours until I prayed for an end to it all.

Those monsters were cowards. They only ever made their presence felt in the dead of night when no one else was around to see.

All I could hope for were fresh memories, fresh thoughts to wash me clean.

A new dawn. A new life.

CHAPTER THIRTY TWO

Next morning I woke up tired and irritable. I decided to check in with Mike, see what I'd missed after I'd left the party last night. When he picked up he sounded groggy, not quite with it, spaced out.

"Hi Sam. Where did you get to last night?"

"Sorry. Too much drink. Someone should have stopped me. What about you? Have a good night?"

I knew he had... I'd watched a lot of it from the shadows.

"You wouldn't believe me if I told you. What can I do for you this fine Saturday morning?"

There was nothing fine about it in my grizzled weary view.

"I was just wondering whether you spoke to Heather and Jamie yesterday. I might be seeing her today and it'd be good to know what I'm facing."

I had no intention of seeing H today, nor any other day if it came to that.

But I did want to know what was on his mind following his Q&A session with her.

"She held the party line like she did with you. As far as she's concerned Jamie misspoke, simple as that. So for now we're no further forward. Good looking woman though isn't she? You said you're seeing her again? Because it'd be good if you did. Try and get behind that bravado, find out what she's hiding."

I thought about that and realised he was right. I still had a better chance of getting a handle on her truth using my more unorthodox approach, my more random methods.

"Okay, I'll see what I can do."

We talked trivia for a short while; he mentioned how pleased Annie was to meet me. And I mentioned how pleased I was that she was pleased. What I didn't tell him was that from what I remembered she was even better looking than him. Instead I agreed to report back as and when I had more information.

I put the phone down wondering how I could get that done, given last night's debacle.

There was nothing else for it. I had to apologise. I called Heather later that morning, script ready, remorseful voice to hand. It took a while for her to pick up, but finally she was there on the other end of the line.

"Hello H. I called to say sorry for my behaviour last night. I was callous, uncaring and insensitive and for that I can only apologise. I thought we might have lunch so I could tell you in person. And because I like looking at you. I could get us a table at Mr Chow's if you want?"

The line was quiet for a while. Then she replied.

"You're a prick. I didn't deserve any of that shit and so soon after Flick's death. What on earth were you thinking?"

"I don't know. Let me apologise face to face. One o'clock at the restaurant?"

She reluctantly agreed, but only after flushing a slurry of insults down the line and they were only partly in jest.

But in the end there I was, back in play.

Mr Chow's was a fifty-year-old Chinese restaurant buried in the heart of Knightsbridge, still serving terrific oriental food to the great and the good after all that time. Better still they knew me there, so getting a good table was easy. Getting H to relax in their surroundings might prove a little more difficult. I arrived five minutes before time and was shown to my table. But it was another half an hour before H appeared at the door, stepping inside and giving her fur jacket to the waiting receptionist. I waved and stood as she came over to me. We kissed politely and sat down. The pre-ordered hot sake arrived with the menus, and we clinked cups as we tasted a piece of Far Eastern history.

Given what had happened last time I decided against raising the circumstances surrounding Flick's death, instead opting for tales of high jinks and adventures during a stint I'd had in Hong Kong in a previous life. Eventually she started to relax. To be clear, the excellent banquet of delicious lunchtime delicacies and the endless sake helped things along the way. But finally I felt we were somewhere near where we'd left off before everything went to shit the other night. And my same old feelings of deep attraction were back too.

She told me about her traumatic visit to the funeral director and the details of the meeting, from the style of coffin to the number of doves to be released after the cremation. It seemed to me that was a very expensive and wasteful way to commemorate a death and I mentioned it. But apparently the doves were trained to return to their baskets once they'd done a couple of circuits of the cemetery. Sort of recycling for profit. The choice of music to 'celebrate her life', as it had been redefined by the parents, had been quite a touchy affair and eventually Mummy and Daddy got their way. Divorced and a long way away on a Zoom call, but still able to work in unison in this very personal family moment. And since they were paying, neither she nor Jamie put up much of a fight.

Things went so well over lunch that Heather invited me back to her place. By now it was mid-afternoon and a couple of gin and tonics later I dared to raise Jamie's slip of the tongue at Joe's again.

"How's Jamie doing at the moment H? I can only imagine the pure hell you're both going through right now. When he ran off he must have been in a proper state. So when he mentioned someone else was here that morning I guess he was just confused, struggling with the enormity of what happened and the impact it's had on the whole family. Strange thing to say though."

I waited, anxious for a positive response, not another flat denial.

H just looked across the coffee table at me and tutted.

"Are we going to have to rehash all that again Sam? Jamie and I spent a very uncomfortable afternoon with Mike Tanner yesterday talking through this whole thing. And he seemed pretty relaxed with our explanation. Why don't you ask him? I know you two get on very well."

She left those words hanging in the air, like bait. I resisted the temptation to bite.

"To tell you the truth H, I'm not sure I know what Mike's thinking nowadays. After all he's not got much to go on has he. It seems to me you've nothing to worry about though. It looks like a bad family row gone horribly wrong doesn't it? I mean, you were there and you didn't see anything strange did you?"

She didn't answer but she did offer coffee. I accepted immediately and she got up, walking through to the kitchen to make it.

I was left alone to consider my options. One thing was for sure; this line of questioning was getting me nowhere and we both knew it. But I was very quickly running out of options. I went out onto the balcony to get some air and clear my head. And what a view. It was panoramic, breath taking in its span of the great city of London which was visible in all its glory on this crisp cold Saturday afternoon. From the London Eye right across to the National Theatre that winter sun washed over the whole of the South Bank and the artful lifestyles that permeated its very being. And as I was admiring those spectacular views, I looked up above me and saw the surveillance camera sitting snugly in the corner of the ceiling and the wall. Overlooking the whole of the balcony and the street below. Just like the one on my terrace two floors above. Just like the ones on every external balcony in the building, fitted as burglary deterrents by the original contractors.

I went back inside. The coffee came and I tried not to gulp the piping hot Nespresso in my haste to get out of there.

We talked about nothing of any consequence for the next half hour and every minute was excruciating as I desperately sought a reason to leave and get to the digital recordings saved from that camera. I have no idea what we talked about, but finally I was able to break away, excusing myself by pretending I'd got an urgent text calling me back to the office.

Once outside her flat, not trusting the lift's speed of response I raced the nine floors down the stairs to the receptionist's office on the ground floor, nearly breaking the door down as I charged into Dougie's domain. He was there, lurking behind a giant slice of pizza.

"Hi Dougie. Sorry to bother you at the weekend like this, but do you know where the tapes for the balcony surveillance cameras are kept?"

He finished chewing his mouthful of pepperoni before replying.

"They're all held digitally. We keep them in the store room behind me." He pointed to a door in the corner of his office.

"What are you looking for?"

"Last week's footage for apartment 9C would be a good start. The owner wants to see it."

"Ah yes. Ms Scott's place? The police took those digital files yesterday. The guy who picked them up was called Tanner I think."

Really.

CHAPTER THIRTY THREE

I got the lift back up to my place and threw myself on the sofa having serviced myself with a large Jack Daniel's and coke for company.

So what was Mike Tanner playing at? Right from the get go there'd been something not quite right about that man. From his outlandish outfit when we first met, to his workplace luxury and his dynamic sex appeal, this was a man apart. And yet up until now I had regarded him as wholly trustworthy. Presumably, he didn't feel the same way about me.

What was on those digital files? Surely if it was anything incriminating he would have already made his move? And why hadn't he told me? If he wanted me to do some digging around, he surely had a duty to keep me informed about matters as serious as evidential film of the scene of the crime that Monday morning?

And another thing. What was a high ranking detective chief inspector doing working solo on this case anyway? They normally hunted in pairs. It was as if he was accumulating evidence for other reasons, reasons unknown to me. I decided to confront him with my concerns.

I dropped him a voicemail asking for a meet first thing Monday morning. That just left me and the weekend to get through.

I called Katey again, but still no luck. I left another message threatening her with death if I didn't get my coat back and settled down to enjoy the rest of my weekend nude and drunk, the TV my only companion.

Just Netflix, me, JD and those deadly night demons to prepare for.

CHAPTER THIRTY FOUR

Monday morning eventually came around and found Betty and me struggling through the cloying, choking, early morning traffic congested all the way to Scotland Yard. The duty officer recognised me and my trusty rust bucket for what we were and called ahead, begging permission to let us through and put him out of his misery. We were obviously an embarrassment to his shiny new building. Someone else agreed with his assessment because permission was granted in short order. Once again Mike was at the lift doors waiting for me and once again I was introduced to the best view in London of London. Croissants, toast and coffee were on offer, so ten minutes later I was dripping marmalade and pastry flakes on my shirt like a true pro.

"Good weekend?" Mike asked me through a mouthful of toast.

"No, not really Mike."

I told him about my weekend discoveries. He stopped eating and listened attentively, slurping coffee and brushing crumbs off his tie while I rattled on. When I was done there was only one question I had left to ask.

"So what I want to know Mike, is what's on those digital files?"

He looked sheepishly at me as if he wasn't sure how to answer or what to say. Then he made up his mind.

"Are you familiar with fixed term Government backed bonds?"

Of course I was. During my time in the City we often joked at what an easy ride those guaranteed bond traders had. Because the lending under those bond terms was guaranteed by the Government of the day. And that was so even if the seller defaulted and was unable to repay the lender. The trading margins were slim, but the volumes were huge, given they were some of the safest investments available in the market.

I confirmed I knew what Government backed bonds were. There may have even been a sneer of condescension in my voice as I did.

Mike took my obvious disdain in his stride.

"Well Peter Waldhan heads up Boerman's Private Banking Bond Investments. And they're the leading City institution selling those bonds in the United Kingdom. Boerman's Bank have a reputation beyond reproach. They've been selling those bond securities since the back end of the nineteenth century and they guard that reputation jealously. Anyway, Peter Waldhan liked their products so much he decided to branch out on his own. So he's put together a crew of professional fraudsters who are issuing fake bonds to all and sundry, using Boerman's name as cover. He's already generated about five hundred million pounds doing it. Boerman's found out what he's been up to when they found errors in their security protocols and procedures. But they can't prove it. I was seconded to the case from homicide. My job is to gather as much evidence as I can to support criminal charges against Waldhan and his cronies. And that includes the Scott family who've been recruited by Peter to sell fraudulent bonds to an unwitting ready market in the leafy lanes of South West London. They've been doing it for the last six months. And now it's a murder enquiry. Which is handy because that's my speciality. Felicity's dead and the camera files shed light on who might have killed her. Would you like to see them?"

I nodded dumbly. That's because I was dumbstruck. I stared across the table at Mike, completely stunned by the news I'd just heard. Mike called his secretary on the intercom and five minutes later we were sat in front of his huge presentation screen situated at the end of his huge office, waiting for his huge show to begin. He dimmed the lights, pressed the 'play' button and the room was instantly dark. Nothing else.

The screen was showing a still shot of H's balcony with a digital clock counter in the bottom right corner of the film denoting the time and date. It was six thirty in the morning on the twenty fourth of November. And absolutely nothing was happening. Except in my head, where questions were marauding around, screaming for answers. What was the real relationship between the Scotts and the Waldhans? How had they got sucked into Peter's fraud? Why was Jamie trying to prise Jenny away from Peter if he was working for him at the same time? And what had any of this to do with Flick's untimely demise?

That screen stillness might provide the answers, or at least some of them.

We too were motionless, waiting for something, anything to break out on screen. Then just as I was getting agitated there was movement. A rerun of that fateful morning had begun right before my eyes. And though it was dark early morning on that balcony, though the film was very grainy and indistinct and though it was shot without the benefit of colour, it was going to give up a whole load of information. I hoped.

We saw the balcony sliding door easing back along its runners as the white tee-shirted back of a large man appeared, hunched over, dragging a body through the gap. He'd locked himself around the torso under the arms to get better purchase. His head was down over the body and the shots were all shades of grey, so it was impossible to tell who he was. Except that he was big and his well-defined back muscles strained at the effort of lifting the body. He was clearly struggling with the dead weight he was manhandling. Eventually he got the body fully out onto the balcony proper and let it fall to the ground in a heap. Still no face shot of him. But the head of the body rolled over on the tiles, in full view at last.

It was Flick.

She lay there still, arms and legs spread-eagled as the man disappeared off camera and back inside. The doors closed again behind him. Excruciatingly motionless film moments passed but lasted only seconds, then the sight of the door reopening and the balcony suddenly had two people on it, milling around. They were looking down so both faces were again hidden from view but judging by her relatively slight frame I was guessing the second figure was that of a woman. It was impossible to be sure because the pictures were too indistinct. All the film was like this; dimly lit, dark and colourless. Also her hair hung loose over her face giving no clue as to her identity. She bent over the body and opened Flick's hand, placing a kitchen knife in it. Flick was oblivious to everything, still as stone. As they leaned over her I was desperate to get just one clean face shot, but that didn't happen. Their body angles meant it was impossible to get any clue who they were. And the picture was so grainy it was a pointless task trying to make out any features. I wondered why such poor surveillance equipment had been installed in the first place. Perhaps it was as old as the building, but whatever the reason it was struggling to do its job. And it only had one job. Back on the balcony the two grainy grey characters were bent over Flick, the woman holding Flick's knees while the man resumed post holding Flick under her arms as they lifted her dead weight up and onto the balcony rail. Then with a final flourish they flipped her over the edge and withdrew into the apartment without even looking back to check their work. Still no obvious clue as to who they were. We saw the terrace door sliding closed and at the same time I imagined the dull thud as Flick's body landed nine floors below. The balcony was motionless once again. So was I. That imaginary thud was going to stay with me for the rest of my life, along with my memory of her lying on the pavement.

The digital clock in the corner of the screen read six thirty-five.

I looked on, grim faced. Mike poured some iced water for us both. We sat staring at each other in the deathly quiet of that room. There were no words. Not for what I'd just witnessed.

Mike broke the baleful silence.

"It's not over yet. Hold on."

I did as I was told, waiting in dread anticipation, yet not knowing why. The digital clock clicked on a notch, then another. Finally, at six thirty-eight the sliding door opened quickly again and we saw Jamie rushing to the balcony rail. Even in that appalling grey light he looked awful. His face betrayed his horror as he looked over the rail and then back inside the flat. A few seconds later a dishevelled looking Heather appeared beside him to peer over the rail and down below. She put her hands to her face and though there was no sound track, she was clearly screaming. A few seconds later and they were gone inside again. Mike stopped the tape.

"And that's it. There is no more. What do you make of it? Is that Jamie and Heather throwing their sister over the rail? It's definitely Jamie and Heather gawking at Felicity's body on the pavement a couple of minutes later.

"When you see the tape it's difficult to see past the fact that both Jamie and Heather admit to being in the apartment on the morning of the fall. And that the two people manhandling Felicity in the footage bear some resemblance to them both. Plus the fact that Jamie let slip there was someone else other than just him and Felicity in the lounge that morning. So they are now prime murder suspects. The trouble is that to get there, to reach that conclusion, you have to also accept that they were so callous they killed their sister and then disposed of her body in such a way as to make it appear like an accident. A sister who by all accounts was a pivotal force in her family's affairs, much loved and admired by both Jamie and Heather. We've interviewed the parents who gave us a pretty clear indication as to who ran the sibling finances in London, how central she was to their London lives.

"Finally you have to decide that they did what they did in full view of the surveillance system, a system designed to stop any wrong doing, recording their every move. They must have known about it.

"Let me ask you something. When you bought the penthouse upstairs, were you informed of the special security measures in place?"

Of course I was. Knight Frank's agent made a big play of it when showing me around. She'd even quipped about it at the time: 'Smile please, you're on Candid Camera'. The joke was so bad I remembered it.

"Then we've got the problem of motive. If they killed her then why? The guy in that footage is big and strong. So's Peter Waldhan. The woman's slight and light; so is Jenny Waldhan. What if it's them throwing her off the balcony? In fact she may have died before then and the whole story about it being a tragic accident was an attempted cover up.

"Whoever those two were, they didn't know about the camera. So neither would they have known they were being watched would they? Or if they did then they didn't care. I don't know. But I do know Peter Waldhan had plenty of motive. As far as he was concerned the Scott family had wronged him on several counts. First off they'd tried to defraud him. Second and just as important, when they couldn't get their own way with the money they'd swindled Felicity tried to engineer the breakup of his marriage.

"I've been over that film several times and it's got me nowhere productive. Except that Jamie and Heather Scott have got some serious questions to answer. But before I pull them in again, I want you to give Heather one last go, see if you can come up with anything that give us a better understanding of what went down that morning. Because right now Heather and Jamie are in a lot of trouble.

"So, are you going to help?"

Help him? Help him? I was still trying to help myself. Still trying to unhear that imaginary soft squelchy dull thud. Still trying to unsee Flick's dead squashed body on the pavement that morning when I went to work.

I had nothing for Mike right now. I still needed to process what I'd just seen, and that wasn't going to be easy. I looked across at him.

"I'm going home, get my head straight. Can I give you a call later?"

We agreed to meet at my offices the next day.

I drove back to Chelsea in a daze.

CHAPTER THIRTY FIVE

It was eleven o'clock when I got back to my offices. In my desk drawer was my secret Jack Daniel's stash. I desperately needed a friend right now and Jack was there for me, as always. I pulled out a dusty plastic cup I found nestling in a multipack next to the bottle, sat back in my chair and filled it full of bourbon. I drank half and cradled the rest in my hands.

So I was simply a pawn in a much larger chess game. And I didn't have the game plan. Flick, Heather and Jamie had, they all knew the game strategy and I'd been sacrificed very early on. By telling Jenny about what the Scotts were up to I had unwittingly set off a train of events over which I had no knowledge and even less control. Flick, Heather and Jamie's plan to get paid out on the back of Jenny's divorce settlement had failed spectacularly when Jenny declared she wanted none of Peter's money.

And a few days after that Flick was just another fly tipping complaint for the Royal Borough of Kensington and Chelsea to clean up. I took another slug, recharging my thin plastic cup.

It was a fair bet that Flick was already dead when she was dragged out onto the balcony. Certainly, the body showed no signs of life at any time during the gruesome disposal process. And by the state of the apartment when the police arrived, there'd been a ferocious struggle in the lounge before she ended up on the pavement nine storeys below. The knife found next to her was obviously a decoy. It was planted on her before she was heaved over the balcony rail. Which meant Jamie had lied about being chased around the lounge. The footage clearly demonstrated that. So I had to agree with Mike. The killing was unlawful and most likely premeditated. And the Scotts were right in the frame. Apart from a motive.

But on the other hand Peter Waldhan had enough motive for them both. Flick and her family had hijacked his Boerman's fraud scam and then embraced it as their own. And tried to collapse his marriage at the same time.

He had a similar build to that of the man in those grainy balcony shots. And Peter wouldn't know he was being filmed. On the other hand, Jamie was built like a brick shithouse as well. And the fact that he was Flick's brother didn't preclude him from her murder. Or the subsequent attempted cover up. And who was that female accomplice featuring so prominently?

That dull grey digital footage was hiding a multitude of sins. All in all that digital history of recent events had a lot to answer for.

By this time Mr Daniel's was in the mood to pipe up with an idea of his own. It came to him as I was helping him into my flimsy plastic beaker again. Maybe Flick had been murdered by aliens cunningly disguised as humans. All part of a larger galactic plot. And maybe not. Either way this back of the envelope office analysis was getting me nowhere but drunk.

I went home to bed and waited for another visit from those demons of mine... I was getting to know them far too well.

CHAPTER THIRTY SIX

The throbbing hangover eventually woke me. It was six that night and I was spread-eagled, naked, sprawled across my bed. I got up and planted myself in the shower, but not before I'd checked my voicemails for evidence I was still alive. There was one from Katey. and she was teasing me to come and get my coat. The excuse was, there were friends and family round for supper.

But she could wait. I needed to wash away what I'd seen in Mike's offices earlier that day.

Two hours later and I was in Fulham. I was so scared of my own company I was sat in Katey's terraced two-up-two-down waiting for food. And whatever else this unusual evening had to bring. She'd arranged an impromptu dinner party for friends and family, that much I knew. But I had no idea why or who. After all I'd only known her a couple minutes and fucked her several times one night when I was pissed. I had no allegiance to this woman.

But I did want my coat back.

Anyway, I was never very good in that forced social setting unless I was truly off my face and I no longer cared. Unfortunately tonight wasn't one of those nights. My body refused to be mistreated again and was using the tried and tested hangover as its means of communication.

The introductions began. I met Melanie and Troy, a mixed couple relationship doomed to failure because he refused to acknowledge his ethnicity. Then there was Tracy and Mark who had two kids under three. Mark had a grey, haunted look about him; like the Grim Reaper was right behind him just waiting for his moment. At the end of the roll call were Doris and Bert, Katey's working-class and massively judgemental parents.

What could possibly go wrong?

I thought I was on safe ground with Katey's mum and dad, so I struck up a conversation asking where they lived and ten seconds later I was being interrogated by Bert about what future there was for a man in my line of work.

I extricated myself by admitting I was a total failure and moved on to the only other parents in the room, Tracy and Mark. Unfortunately, my knowledge of the price gap between Aldi's and Tesco's nappies let me down, as did my understanding of the dilemmas of getting tiny children placed in suitable state education and how it affected where you lived. As a consequence, Tracey and I had very little in common and Mark wasn't doing any talking at all. He was too afraid to speak without her permission. In any case he knew he'd let her down as a matter of principle and matrimonial experience, so he deferred to her judgement on all family matters. Life was easier that way.

That left me and Troy coming to terms with why black lives mattered more than anyone else's. My point that adding the word 'equally' to the slogan might have cleared up any confusion was drowned out in a welter of misinformed abuse. Even though Troy was white, having changed his name by deed poll in a gesture of solidarity with the movement.

By dessert I was thinking about topping myself. And I'd changed my mind about not drinking for the night.

Finally the evening was over and despite Katey's pleadings for me to stay I left with the others. I went on my way wishing them all well, while at the same time silently vowing never to see any of them ever again.

All apart from Katey. And that was only a maybe.

But at least I made sure I made my escape with my coat safely under my arm.

I decided to walk back to Chelsea and fifteen minutes later I was outside my apartment door. But as I approached I realised I wasn't the only one there.

Mike Tanner, looking very much the worst for wear, was leaning against my doorframe, blood trickling from the back of his head. I grabbed him by the arm and pulled him inside, ushering him over to the couch. I got some ice and chilled water from the fridge door, grabbed a tea towel and hurried back to the lounge. But he was already beyond my reach. Slumped down on the sofa with his head perched delicately on a cushion, his hanky placed carefully underneath the bleeding, he was breathing deeply, slowly, rhythmically. He was going nowhere. I removed his shoes and lifted his legs up onto his impromptu bed. I found a spare duvet and that was him settled for the rest of the night.

When I woke next morning there was a lot of noise over in the kitchen area. I could smell bacon, even heard it sizzling in the pan. I grabbed my dressing gown and went to investigate.

The kitchen was a hive of cooking activity with coffee percolating, toast popping, eggs frying. The counter was set for a good old fashioned English breakfast. Put simply, Mike was busy making a feast. He grunted when I appeared and waved me over to my place-setting, pouring a fresh orange juice for me as I sat down. His face was clean shaven and bloodless, ready to face the worst or best the day had to offer. Unlike me. Before I could open up a conversation the food arrived on the counter staring up at me, begging to be devoured. And I was definitely in the mood to comply. It must have been five minutes before either of us lifted our faces out of our plates. I felt the need to say something.

"Morning Mike. Great start to the day. Thanks for the breakfast. Everything else okay in your world?"

He smiled at my probe into his personal affairs.

"My way of thanking you for last night's hospitality. At least we won't have to meet later this morning."

He looked back down at the remains of his food and set about finishing it. No explanation. Nothing. Just the scraping of his knife on his plate as he went hunting down the remaining baked beans. I tried again.

"Anything else you want to talk about?"

No reply, just that scraping and the intermittent silence that went with it while he chewed his food. When he'd finished, he got up and came around the kitchen aisle clearing plates and condiments as he went. Only when he'd finished and loaded the dishwasher did he come over to me and sit down on the next stool.

"It was my turn on Jamie duty last night. I followed him back from the gym about ten o'clock, then I lost sight of him in the basement car park. When I got out of my car to go find him something hit me on the back of my head and I went down. That's all I remember. When I came to I recalled our first meeting when you said you lived above Heather in the penthouse, so I flashed my credentials at Dougie and he let me up to your floor. Hope you don't mind? Never saw who did it and that part of the carpark's a blind spot, so no way of knowing from surveillance cameras. Dougie apologised though. But I was hit hard."

He was rubbing the back of his head, but he looked okay to me. Those beautiful, bright, wide-awake eyes gave him away.

"So what are you going to do about it?"

"Not sure yet. I don't want to pull Jamie. I've got no evidence he did it and anyway I'd have to explain what I was doing in the carpark following him, wouldn't I? But don't worry about Jamie. I've got plans for him. He may have blown my cover, but soon that's going to be the very least of his problems."

He smiled again, but this time it was an ugly, menacing smile and whatever it was he had planned for Jamie, I didn't want to know. But I did want to talk about what I'd seen at Mike's offices the previous day.

"Listen, I've been thinking about your little floorshow yesterday and I've come up with some observations."

I covered the thoughts I'd had in my office. I also included some of the more random ones I'd had in a drunken haze later at home. I talked about the size of the man doing the heavy lifting on the balcony and how it might have been Peter. But equally it could have been Jamie apart from the fact that he was her brother. As for the woman in view, well I had no idea. Could be Heather, could be Jenny, could be anyone. Family ties made H an unlikely candidate in my view. And anyway, she had no reason. Privately I wondered how much those thoughts had to do with my feelings for her rather than the evidence as it presented itself.

Other than that I had nothing. Nor had Mike. Which I mentioned was a worry given he was the principal investigating officer.

"I'm calling both the Scotts in for further questioning. But before I do, will you speak to Heather? Try and make yourself a part of her life. Talk to her again one last time. She's at the centre of all this mess. She's Jamie's sister. She's also a part of Peter's South West London fraud ring, she was in the flat the morning Felicity fell and she's already told you she wanted Peter and Jenny divorced so her brother could get his hands on the divorce money from them. We need a breath of fresh air over all this, so just keep trying to give us a new perspective and see what you come up with."

Given my last outing with H, I seriously doubted there was anything in the air between us but a bad smell. But once again Mike was insistent that this was the best way forward and so once again I agreed to do the needful. When he left his parting words were ringing in my ears.

"You've got until tomorrow morning to come up with something."

CHAPTER THIRTY SEVEN

By the time I got to my office I knew I had a full day ahead. Maggie was already there telling me Heather and Jamie were coming over at eleven to speak privately with me. I had no idea what that meant, so I busied myself with cruising through the early rounds of my latest darts tournament qualifier with Eric Bristow and the clock. As it chimed eleven, the intercom buzzed and Maggie was on the other end announcing Heather and Jamie's arrival. Maggie followed them through with a tray of coffee and then the three of us were left alone. The two of them sat across from me, looking decidedly uncomfortable. Jamie spoke first.

"Look Dickhead. I'm being followed by the Police. And I don't like it. Do you know why it's happening?"

Well yes, I had a pretty good idea, but he didn't need to know that.

"No I don't. But I could hazard a guess. It might have something to do with the fact that you tried to embezzle money from the Waldhans, the both of you, mightn't it? Oh yes and let's not forget the small matter of the body found on the pavement, nine floors below your apartment with both you there when she fell."

I was staring them squarely in the face, looking for any signs of weakness. H looked away first and coloured up. But Jamie was defiant.

"Anyway, there'll be one less plod following me today. I made sure of that last night. He made the mistake of following me into my basement carpark where the lights are dim, and the cameras don't see so well."

The wicked smile on his face meant he didn't even know who he'd clubbed from behind. Idiot.

"You're a bum chum of Tanner's, aren't you? Go find out what's on his mind. How much'll it cost me?"

I thought it was about time I put an end to his ritual abuse.

"You don't like me much do you Jamie? Not even when you come crawling for my help. So you'd better give me one good reason why I should do anything for you ever, Tosser."

He bristled at the reminder of that lunchtime at the Waldhans and the repeated insults he'd had to take from Peter. He looked out of the window at the winter sky above. Then he looked back.

"Okay Sam, maybe I've been a bit hard on you. But I don't like you sniffing around my family looking for trouble. And I particularly don't like you trying to get into my sister's knickers. But this is different. My love for Jenny was real enough at the start; it just went stale over time. And as for Felicity, well I've told Tanner everything I know about that. I shouldn't have run away, I know that too. But that doesn't make me a murderer does it? Will you help us or not?"

Then it was Heather's turn.

"We don't really know where else to turn Sam."

She stretched her hand across the desk and it touched mine. That touch lingered a long time after they'd both left the building. But it had the desired effect.

"I'll see what I can do."

Of course I knew what was going on, but this was an easy way into the secret life of the Scotts, me as their confidante, working in their best interests against what they saw as police intrusion into their private lives. I called Mike and updated him.

"Excellent. Time to turn up the heat then."

Sure enough Jamie was on the phone later that afternoon complaining about police harassment.

"When I left your offices I picked up a shadow. He followed me everywhere I went. He even waved to me at one point, just to make sure I knew he was there. Then this afternoon I was pulled over by a Met Police patrol car on the street. The mobile plod accused me of having defective tail lights and when I got out to look, he broke one of them with the back of his taser. Then he pointed it at me and smiled as he issued his mandatory caution. Wanker. What do you think?"

What I thought was that Mike was being true to his word over breakfast.

"They're just trying to rattle you Jamie. Stay calm and I'll keep digging. Is Heather okay?"

She was with him, so he put her on the 'phone.

"What can we do Sam? I'm seeing policemen behind every tree."

"Leave it with me. I'll talk to Tanner right away."

I hung up and called Mike to congratulate him.

"Well, you've really got them both rattled. Probably time to ease off for the day and make me look like their saviour."

"You'll enjoy that, won't you Sam?"

I couldn't deny it and I didn't. Instead I waited for the inevitable call from Jamie early that evening.

"I don't know what you did Sam, but it's all gone quiet for now. Thanks."

"I told Tanner I was working for you and I could save him a job by giving him regular updates on your whereabouts and movements. And he seemed okay with that. But that means you need to tell me what you're up to, within reason."

Jamie agreed, thanked me again and hung up. I was just thinking what a simple naive fool he was if he thought Mike Tanner was ever going to forget what had happened the previous night when the phone rang again. This time it was Heather.

"Thanks Sam, for calling off the dogs. How can I ever repay you?"

I could think of a thousand ways, but I didn't know her well enough yet.

"Dinner?"

We agreed to meet at Daphne's later at eight. Daphne's was a top end local Italian with a huge reputation and a small client register. It was normally very difficult to get a table unless you were on 'the list'. I was, so it wasn't.

I got there five minutes early and waited in the small intimate cocktail area pending Heather's arrival. The barman brought me my usual, but I had time for another before Heather deigned to make an appearance just after eight thirty. It didn't matter though because Gabriel, the maître d', knew me well enough to understand that I never dined there unless it was with a beautiful woman. His job was to go fetch his Latin sexuality and pour on the charm. And he was always more than willing to do that. It was the irrepressible Italian showman in him, bursting to get out.

I nodded his way when she arrived and he was at reception in a shot, oozing grace and suave sophistication. It was as if he'd been waiting all his life to meet her. He welcomed her with a vocal fanfare of Italian excitement, waving his arms and reaching for her with a double cheek kiss. He was being way too familiar, but she didn't seem to mind the attention at all as she followed him over to me. By now the whole restaurant was looking on, wondering who she was to attract such urgent, unwavering devotion to duty. For her part Heather looked slightly uneasy and mildly embarrassed by his naked and highly visible show of affection toward her. But she smiled shyly as she approached. We kissed politely and then it was my turn to follow as Gabriel showed us over to our small intimate window seats. He'd given us that premier space in full view of everyone ambling along the street outside. We were almost a window advertisement inviting the passers-by to come dine with the beautiful people. What a joke.

But if that didn't impress Heather, nothing would.

The truth of the matter was I was totally conflicted where she was concerned. She'd already freely confessed to being part of a conspiracy to install Jamie in Peter Walhan's place. And that it was solely for the purposes of getting hands on Peter's money. Worse, Detective Chief Inspector Mike Tanner believed she was implicated in an elaborate financial fraud involving at least half a billion pounds in embezzled private funds. Last but by no means least, she might also be involved in the death of her sister and the cover up of the crime in her flat only a week ago.

So what was I doing here? Why was I so taken with her? I'd only known her a couple of weeks and I wasn't the sort of bloke who fell hard and fast for any woman I met.

The answer was looking right at me across the dinner table. Under those dimmed lights and by the flickering candlelight, she was simply irresistible. She didn't need any surgery. She didn't need any make-up. She didn't need that fine silk pink and blue floral Chanel dress fitting so snugly around her slender frame. Even her Graff jewellery was superfluous to requirements. All she needed were those crystal clear azure blue eyes and those flowing curled blonde locks sitting recklessly on her shoulders. That porcelain pink skin stretched tight over her high cheek bones and those full, warm, inviting lips suggestively pouting at the slightest opportunity.

They did the trick for her.

In short I was in trouble. Big trouble.

We ordered our food and wine and for some time talked and giggled as we recalled Gabriel's absurdly extravagant behaviour when she'd walked in. Meanwhile that soft, left bank Parisian blues jazz floated across the room, mingling with the low hum of lovers whispering their most intimate secrets to one another.

I poured her a glass of Corton and decided the moment was right; I needed to come clean. I reached over and stroked her hand.

"Heather, we need to talk. But I don't know how to say what I want to say. The thing is, I'm struggling to deal with some of the stuff you've been up to. I don't how you got involved with the Peter and Jenny Waldhan in the first place. And I don't get why you felt the need to try and wreck their marriage. Even if it's legal, what you did is morally wrong. So why did you do it? Most importantly I need to know the truth about what happened the morning Flick went over the balcony."

I took my hand off hers and took a sip of the cold rich dry white wine. She did the same. There was an awkward silence while she looked me over, as if she were sizing me up for a suit or something. Then finally she sighed, leaned forward and reached for my hand again.

"Okay Sam. Off the record?" I nodded.

"I've done some things I'm not very proud of. And there's some stuff I can't tell you about. But Peter Waldhan is not what he seems. I've been working for him and his company Boerman's for several months now. It all started when Flick was employed as their nanny. She was an instant hit with Jenny Waldhan, and the kids adored her. After a few months she and Peter became good friends too. Flick had spent a brief time working in the City as an intern, so she was naturally interested in his high rolling trader lifestyle. And he was just as interested in her local Chelsea connections, her other clients, our family social network, all of that.

"Eventually he told her about a new product he'd started trading for Boerman's. He asked if she wanted to try it out on her Chelsea contacts. It was commission only work and she'd be self-employed, but the money might be good if she had even a modicum of success in selling bonds.

"She jumped at the chance and the whole thing was an immediate success. Soon she was racking up clients all round here and it became far too much for her to cover alone. She asked Peter if she could involve me and Jamie and he agreed. Three months later, between us we had sold nearly one hundred million pounds worth of bonds. And all at one percent commission. We couldn't believe it. Neither could Peter."

She looked wistfully at me as she remembered those days, but she was teasing her slender fingers around the rim of her glass as she did so.

And that made it very difficult for me to concentrate on what she was saying.

"I remember when we each got our first commission cheques; the champagne flowed all night at the Eclipse that evening. Peter explained from the outset that we would be freelance, self-employed, sole traders selling one of Boerman's most important products on an exclusive basis.

"At first when we saw the commission cheques were made out to and signed off on Peter's personal account we thought nothing of it. The amounts were always right and as far as we were concerned we were trading Boerman's bonds through him.

"But one day Flick's best friend checked the bond registration documents on her investment. There weren't any. When she contacted Boerman's she quickly established her guaranteed bonds so famously trailed as being backed by the Government, were no such thing. Boerman's didn't recognise them, they weren't registered with them and therefore they were unsecured. No Government guarantee attached to her investments at all.

"Boerman's were horrified when they realised they'd been misrepresented in this way. But they immediately went into reputational protection mode and refunded her monies immediately to avoid any adverse publicity. In return she agreed to sign a non-disclosure agreement. And then promptly told Flick what had happened anyway.

"We realised we'd been played by Peter. We didn't know he was committing a fraud on Boerman's when we started. We were innocent.

But when we confronted him he refused to pay us our commissions and threatened to take us down with him if he was caught. We'd done nothing wrong but we felt like criminals. That's when we took affirmative action. We decided to continue selling his bonds but this time we set up our own bank account for cash collections. We knew what we were doing was illegal, but the money was irresistible. We used Boerman's name, just as Peter had, but using a limited liability partnership in the company acronym – B.G.L.LLP. So we were selling the same products but diverting the money into our account rather than his. At the same time, because Jenny and Jamie were already an item and she was so in love, we hatched the hair brained scheme to punish Peter and get our residual commissions a different way.

"It was stupid I know. And it was doomed to failure. But it was all going really well until Peter found out. He was furious, incandescent with rage. He threatened to shop us unless we stopped."

Heather paused as if to give me a minute to soak it all in. I was going to need more than a minute.

"So what happened that morning in your flat?"

H took another drink.

"That's the bit I can't tell you about. But I can tell you that we had nothing to do with Flick's death."

There was a deeply defiant angry look in her eyes as she stared over at me, daring me to challenge her version of events.

Which was never going to happen. But dinner was effectively over.

Along with any pretence I didn't care for this woman.

CHAPTER THIRTY EIGHT

I called Mike the next morning to report back on the previous evening's events. But even as he was picking up I could hear his laughter down the other end of the line.

"I've got to tell you about what just happened." He could hardly contain himself as he continued. "Jamie just called in to report his Mercedes was stolen. We had to inform him that it'd been impounded for illegal parking outside the gym he uses. Apparently he threw a hissy fit when he was told it was in the Perivale pound, out by the Hoover Building ten miles away. And he was looking at a three hundred quid release fine plus recovery costs totalling another four hundred. The duty officer at the local Chelsea station said the language was pretty ripe. So you don't need to tell me where Jamie is today... I already know."

He started chuckling again and I couldn't help thinking Jamie was in a whole world of trouble now he was Mike's plaything. Eventually, after he'd calmed down, I put in my report. When I was finished he wasn't laughing any more.

"Do you believe her when she says she didn't know she was selling bent bonds initially?"

I had to think about that one.

"Yes, I think I do. It's certainly possible. Otherwise what she did to try and recover her commission money makes no sense. The whole family were clearly incensed by Peter's treatment of them, enough to go to extreme lengths to get their fees back. I don't think they'd have done that if they were complicit in the original crime. They'd have kept their mouths shut and walked away, wouldn't they?"

"That's true enough. But if they were ignorant of Waldhan's original criminal activities then why didn't they come and tell us when they knew what was going on? They were innocent at that stage. What did they have to lose?"

I thought about that for a moment.

"Nothing. Except the money from the new clients they'd signed up. I don't know Mike, the whole thing's so very confusing." But Mike was anxious to press on with his assessment.

"And why on earth did they start up their own scam using Peter's model? They were always going to get caught out. They had no direct connection to Boerman's bank. It was Peter who gave them those credentials. Without him they had nothing. Total amateurs.

"And then there's the camera footage. That clearly shows two people throwing Felicity off the balcony at six thirty-five that morning. Whoever they were, they had to have access to the apartment. There were no signs of forced entry and anyway Heather and Jamie lived there for fuck's sake. It's their flat.

"Then, to top it all off, Jamie escapes the crime scene and goes on the run.

"To me that makes them prime suspects, whatever Heather says. I'm afraid I'm going to have to bring them in and press charges Sam."

My heart sank. Because Mike was right. They were both there that morning and two characters looking very much like them were filmed disposing of Flick's body. That was enough evidence to begin a murder case enquiry and they had to be the two most likely candidates.

CHAPTER THIRTY NINE

Jamie and Heather were picked up and arrested for fraud and suspected murder later that morning. The fraud case depended on many recorded and well documented events. The murder case on the other hand was largely centred around that really incriminating film evidence. This was shown to Heather and Jamie in support of the arrests being made. But bail was going to be an issue. The courts didn't like letting suspected murderers back out on the streets. It gave out the wrong impression. It wasn't a good look and the public didn't like it.

I found them at Charing Cross Police Station later that day, after they'd been questioned and I'd suffered a turgid taxi ride across town. I could have walked faster. They were being held separately so I asked to see Heather first. Surprisingly, I was familiar with the inside of a police station so I'm not sure what I expected to see when I walked into the visitors' reception area. But it surely wasn't this.

Pale green washed walls, Formica tables with metal benches all screwed to the floor, large black and white chequered lino lifting up at the edges. And the all-pervading sense of crushed dreams, shattered illusions all folded in with the heavily oppressive atmosphere of raw fear.

Heather was sat over in the corner, blonde hair scraped back off her pale tearstained face. She was wearing faded white one piece overalls and canvas slippers. No jewellery. Just looking very tired. And small. And insignificant.

I squeezed into the bench space opposite her and looking up I recognised the duty officer who'd ushered me in. He was standing by the door filling the exit. There'd be no privacy for us today then.

"Hello Heather. How are you?" As I spoke I was wishing I hadn't on at least two counts.

First it was a completely inane question to ask this beautiful woman, a woman who'd never been near a police station in her whole life, how she was doing in jail. What self-respecting, drop-dead gorgeous female would ever want to make an enforced visit to Charing Cross Police Station as the number one suspect in a murder case? How did I think she was doing? What a prick.

Second, her tears started to flow as soon as I opened my fat mouth. They slid gracefully, softly down her pale cheeks onto the grey plastic table top as she looked over at me, searching for the words to express her pain. I gulped back my own feelings at seeing her like this, trapped in her own silent misery. At last she spoke.

"I saw camera footage of Flick going over the balcony today."

And in that moment she was totally vulnerable, exposed, drowning in her own fear. I answered easily and with conviction.

"I'm there for you Heather. I'll get to the bottom of this. Have you got a lawyer? I know a really good one, he was best man at my wedding and he specialises in criminal law. In fact he's the one I've got to blame for getting me started in this line of work."

My weak insipid smile evoked no discernible response. I just hoped I sounded convincing. She was busy counting the bars on the three feet by two feet window that offered the only natural light into the room. There were only four bars, but it was taking an inordinately long time for her to count them. The tears had stopped, and I could see the trace lines they had left on her face as the daylight fell through the bars. She turned to me.

"Have you seen that footage?"

I explained I had, the previous day. Her face was etched with grief as the memories of what she'd seen came flooding back.

"It was almost too hard to watch. Just thrown over the side to fall nine floors down to the pavement below. Like a sack of potatoes.

"I don't need your mate. I've retained Gordon Calloway. Jamie and I saw him earlier. He's going to want to speak with you too. I've told him everything I know and so should you. I've also told him you're investigating Flick's death on our behalf. Is that okay?"

She sounded so desperate.

I nodded my approval. Truth be known, a part of me was relieved she'd let me in, let me try and help her. Another part of me wondered whether I could help her at all. I knew that name Calloway. He was legend in the field of criminal law as it goes and his record as a criminal defence lawyer was first class. I told her so.

But there was something different between Heather and me today. Last night's soft romance was replaced with a new harsh reality, a reality neither of us was dealing with very well. The chat was polite, courteous, friendly even. But the sparkle was gone from her eyes. That sparkle I yearned for. I began to realise, for the first time, that I must help this woman in a practical sense. That's what she needed right now, not gentle platitudes of moral support. And I had no idea how to do that.

We said our goodbyes and as I kissed her I promised again to try and help. She just looked straight through me, nodding but clearly not believing a word.

Next up was Jamie. I stayed where I was and five minutes later he was sat opposite me, shaking my hand vigorously.

"Great to see you Sam. Thanks for coming down to see us."

I was surprised by the enthusiasm behind his greeting given his general demeanour towards me at every previous meeting between us. That and the fact that he was up on a murder charge supported by clear and unambiguous evidence that at the very least he and Heather had lied to the police. The video footage told its own story.

"How's it going Jamie?" He too was dressed for the occasion, with statutory white overalls and canvas shoes. But somehow he was in a different place to Heather.

"It's all good. My lawyer says he'll have us out in forty-eight hours or sooner. He says they've got no case against us that'll stand up in court and he's putting the champagne on ice!"

And there was the difference between Jamie and Heather, summed up by his reaction to being locked up as compared to hers. He saw his incarceration as a little local difficulty waiting to be fixed by Mr Golden Bollocks Calloway. H, on the other hand, saw it for what it was; deadly serious.

I had very little else of any consequence to say to this chimp, so I checked he was okay, got a list of stuff he needed to make his life more bearable then listened to his childlike understanding of his position for a short while. But I couldn't deal with his juvenile, simplistic view of his world for very long. So soon I said my goodbyes and made my way out into the fresh air. And I needed lungful's of it.

What a waste of time that had been. I walked across Trafalgar Square aiming kicks at the hosts of pigeons pecking for the imaginary food at my feet. I missed every time. They'd seen it all before. Nevertheless I was soon drawing unwelcome attention from the animal welfare brigade, so I shuffled away seeking out some other defenceless group of innocent bystanders to take my frustrations out on. All I found down Whitehall was a group of Japanese tourists taking pictures of the solitary Queen's Guardsman standing to point outside his sentry box.

But he was carrying a loaded rifle, so I walked on by.

CHAPTER FORTY

It took me an hour to walk back to my office through Green Park. Along the way I was trapped with confused thoughts rattling around in my head and no distractions to stop them.

My frustration lay in the fact that I had no purchase in this murder case. I had nothing to go on and no one new to talk to. All of the available evidence led to the probability that Heather and Jamie had killed their sister and then tried to reframe it as an accident. But there was something about the whole stinking mess that didn't ring true. Why on earth would Jamie and Heather have disposed of Flick's body in the full knowledge that their every move was being captured for eternity on camera? It didn't make sense. Nor why they'd do it in the first place.

And Mike Tanner, for all his outward enthusiasm at having me around, was being of very little practical assistance. Far from it. He was keeping vital evidence from me unless pressed.

I needed an ally. Someone in the know. Someone who could help me unravel the truth, someone who might have inside information.

By the time I walked into my ante room and greeted Maggie I had the germ of an idea.

Scratching around in my desk drawer I found Annie's phone number. She'd given it to me the other night after she'd punched me in the throat. I called her.

"Hello Annie. I'm betting I made such an impression on you last time we met that you haven't forgotten me. Need a clue who I am?"

"Hello Sam. How's your hard on today?"

Simple as that. One day that intro' joke had to work for me and this was that day. The next ten minutes were pure joy if you were a masochist. Once we'd got past my play making ineptitude and moved on from my limited dancing skills, she tormented me with a series of faux pas I'd made that night which she had found absolutely hilarious, sadly none of which I remembered.

The result was a drinks date that evening at the Mandarin Bar on Knightsbridge. Snuggled intimately inside the Mandarin Oriental Hotel, it was my idea of heaven because it was a classy watering hole and an up market pick up joint I knew only too well.

I got there ten minutes ahead of time and settled at my reserved table waving at Silvado, the drinks maestro there. I found it was always a good idea to befriend the incumbent cocktail barman when I was out in Chelsea and Knightsbridge getting slammed. And in this case there wasn't a cocktail Silvado couldn't make, including the best Long Island in town. He nodded his understanding and set about his work.

The place was busy for a Tuesday night, but then the best places were always busy and this was the best of places. Situated adjacent to the entrance to Dinner, the glass walls allowed uninterrupted views of the comings and the goings of the great and the good, if two star Michelin dining was your thing. Alternatively you could relax in the moody seduction created in the bar area, deep sofas casually strewn around the room but always an open reception area into the bar, a semi-circular affair. The bar stools were pushed tight up to it, far too close for discretion when they were all occupied which they usually were. My drink came along with Annie, who'd gone to the bar and been pointed in my general direction by Silvado. The waiter placed my drink and then stepped aside, seeking instruction. I kissed Annie lightly on her cheek and he took her order. We sat down as the waiter disappeared to get her martini cocktail. She was bang on time and I liked that in a woman so I told her.

"Who could miss the opportunity of meeting Sam Cove, the famous joker, the dreadful drunk, the appalling dancer and intrepid womaniser?"

How accurate was that summary? I winced.

She laughed as she settled back into her chair and we looked each other up and down for the first time.

She'd arrived in a one piece midnight black calf length pencil dress, split halfway up her thighs. And as a consequence most of her smooth legs were on show when she moved. So were her slender calves and black three-inch stilettos. The rest of her dress was wrapped tight around her taut body revealing her hard fit frame. The square cut design around her throat was severe, slightly threatening, definitely daring. All in all she was absolutely oozing sexual danger. I kept my eyes on hers, though it was incredibly difficult; her legs were crossed but her knees were on show and I was finding it really hard not to ogle. She swivelled away as her drink arrived and I told the waiter to leave the tab open. I was going to need more drinks.

"So how've you been?" she asked.

"Well, not so good as it goes." I launched into a description of today's events and how helpless I felt. She listened attentively. Then she responded.

"Ah yes, I know a bit about this one. Mike's been bringing it home with him every night. This is about that young Scott woman's death isn't it? Killed and thrown off a balcony wasn't she? Mike let me see the stills from the camera shots. Did you know her?"

Is that what Mike really thought?

Again I was forced to describe my relationship with the Scotts, without going into any sensitive details. But that wouldn't do. Not for Annie.

"Mike says you fancy the dead woman's sister. Is that why you went to see her today?"

So he did, did he? What other thoughts had he shared with her but not with me? What else had he told Annie? I asked her. She shrugged.

"He can't see past that camera footage and the two people shoving that woman over the terrace wall. They looked remarkably like the brother and sister, don't you think? He reckons it's compelling evidence. That and the fact there are no other suspects. What's your angle on all this Sam? And why do you care so much?"

She leaned forward and placed her hand on my thigh. I felt the buzz. I took a drink and leaned into her to get heard above the music. Her scent was sweet and gentle. It was as much as I could do not to kiss her neck as I whispered in her ear.

"There's a couple of things not quite right about all this Annie. For a start, if they did it there's no motive. None that I know of anyway. What the hell happened that was so serious as to drive them to murder their own sister? Second, why would they expose themselves on camera like that? Those of us with terraces, we all complain about the inconvenience. The three monthly checks on the camera hardware are a real bore. That janitor is an absolute nightmare. He drives us nuts, having to hang around and listen to his monosyllabic stories about his dull dreary life while he loiters, pretending he's testing the equipment. He takes forever and he never shuts up. But we all know why that camera's there and we all take great comfort in the extra security it provides. So they must have known they'd be caught on film. Why risk it? That's what I want to know. Making a positive I.D. will be nigh on impossible given the quality of the images, but why would they take that risk? It doesn't make any sense."

The waiter was cruising the room again, looking for action. I stopped talking and ordered our repeat drinks. But then Annie said something which stopped me in my tracks.

"Mike's not sure Heather or Jamie had anything to do with their sister's death. But until he gets to the truth, he's stuck. The only evidence of what happened that morning is on those digital files and they're pretty damning. But right now he's got nowhere else to go. Have you spoken to him about your misgivings?"

"Several times, but he's never mentioned any doubts about their guilt. He could have said something."

Annie may have detected the disappointment in my voice.

"Mike's a very careful man Sam. And he always plays his cards very close to his chest. We've lived in each other's pockets for most of our lives, yet he's quite capable of keeping the most important of things from me. It can be really quite frustrating at times."

Annie was thirty-four but, unlike Mike, she'd finished her expensive education, taken a degree in psychology and was now working as a senior consultant at University College Hospital. They'd always been close growing up, but when Mike got kicked out of school she kept in even closer contact while he went through a tough time with their parents. When she moved to London at nineteen she moved in with him and they'd been together ever since.

"Has Mike ever told you why he had to leave Eton?"

"No."

"It's because he was caught dealing. A regular little pot party he had going there. Half the sixth form were using by the time the school found out. He was instantly dismissed, but the real trouble started when Daddy was told by the Headman. As an old Etonian himself, Father was so appalled and ashamed by Mike's behaviour he threw him out of the family home.

"Mike was in a right state at that time, completely off his face on drugs with no prospects for the future. Daddy refused to help, apart from letting him use our London home as a squat for a few months while he got himself sorted out.

"Anyway, as time went by Mike got help and was becoming less needy. Between us we finally got him off his habit. But during his rehabilitation he decided he wanted to do something about what he'd seen and where he'd been when he was a dealer. So he joined the police. Two years later I came to London to do my degree and I stayed with him. That was seventeen years ago and we're still squatting now. Knightsbridge isn't the worst place to doss down in though. And Mike's found a new way of channelling his energies into cleaning up the streets."

"And his relationship with Mummy and Daddy?"

"Stuck in the past. Father can never forgive him for the embarrassment and shame he brought on the family name. And for his part, Mike's stopped trying to please everyone else. He just pleases himself nowadays."

Annie was idly pushing the crudités around the serving dish on the drinks table, immersed in her private thoughts as they washed over past events.

And while that back catalogue was useful in getting to know more about Mike, it wasn't going to get me anywhere if I was trying to prove Heather's innocence. Was that was I was trying to do? Because if it was, I clearly had a lot of work on my hands.

"So if Mike's got it in his head that the Scotts are being framed, what's he going to do about it?"

I waited to see if she'd give anything away. She looked up at me.

"You haven't answered my question. Why did you see Heather today?"

Hmm... she was right. I hadn't answered her because I didn't really know why I felt the way I did about H. And I was starting to doubt my reasons for wanting to help her. For all I knew she was guilty as sin. Most of the evidence pointed that way. Maybe I was simply unwilling to recognise what was staring me straight in the face. That I had feelings for her.

"Call it professional curiosity. I suppose it's because I knew Flick and I want her killer found."

Of course that was all just so much tosh, but it got me off the hook for now. Annie stood up.

"Well I've had far too much to drink, so it's home time for me. I only live round the corner. Do you fancy a nightcap?"

She looked like she already knew the answer and she was right.

Montpelier Square was indeed a short walk from the Mandarin but I still managed to wrap my Crombie round us both on the way back, purely for the purposes of keeping warm. Well that was my excuse and I was sticking to it.

When we got there, her squat wasn't like any squat I'd ever seen before.

Stepped up from the pavement and guarded by black iron railings across its front, her Grade II listed home was a shrine to old family money and the easy style that flows from it. This Georgian four bedroomed property was probably worth something in excess of seven million and it looked every penny of it. Annie suggested I get acquainted with the place while she fixed us a drink, so I did.

Downstairs the modern interior was in complete contrast to the austere look of the place from the outside. Impressionist art was casually scattered all around. When I wasn't looking at a Dali original on a wall, my eye was drawn by the several bronzes perched on floodlit revolving stands liberally stationed around the room. The one that took my fancy was the statue of Icarus falling from the sky, his wings in meltdown from flying too close to the sun. It reminded me of my City trading days and my fall from grace. But pride of place was given over to a two-foot-long bronze figure of a Minotaur, body positioned in the foetal position, clutching his horns in demented torture. It reminded me of my own inner pain when I remembered how I'd treated my marriage and my wife.

Upstairs each bedroom had been individually designed and named. The master bedroom was called 'The Guild Room' named after Tricia Guild, whereas the guest bedroom was called 'Lauren' after Ralph of that name and so on. The rest of the house was immaculately but tastefully decorated; rolled damask pearl wallpaper acting as a neutral background to the exquisite paintings which adorned the lounge and library areas.

The basement had been a more recent development. Mr Tanner Snr clearly had a penchant for spending time in the kitchen; he'd devoted the complete basement floor space to a cooking, dining and living experience that was quite simply stunning. Split into three sections, at the street end was the dining area comprising a modern square oak dining table with cushioned bench seating on all four sides. Perfect for casual entertaining. The middle section was an open lounge area complete with full Bang and Olufsen designer entertainment system and eight-seater corner sofa. The focal point though was the wall mounted eighty-five-inch plasma screen with surround sound, ideal for home entertainment in almost any form. Then at the far end of the room was the kitchen area. It had a commercial feel to it, with stainless steel splashbacks, four ovens, three fridges, three waste disposals, a dishwasher and a pure quartz central island that was as big as a table tennis table, surrounded by brown leather bar stools. I noted that all the kitchen equipment was Miele. What a place. I was busy opening and closing the fish oven, trying to work out how electricity and water could mix in that closed environment without tragic consequences when Annie returned, drinks in one hand, buff folder in the other.

"Have a look at that and tell me what you think." She slid the file across the counter to me, the title clear to see. It read simply 'Peter Waldhan'.

"What's this?" I sat at the breakfast bar and took a sip of my gin and tonic.

"It's a report detailing his movements over the past three months, ever since Mike took on the case."

I wondered why I was being allowed access to sensitive police information not shown to me when I was at the Yard. The answer was obvious. Mike wanted me to see more stuff I wasn't officially allowed to see. He must have decided I needed a break. He was right.

I took another, bigger slug and opened the file.

It was three o'clock next morning when I left Annie's place and walked the cold empty streets back home. I was in a dark, sombre mood and I needed to feel the biting wind in my face.

That file had been a fascinating read.

CHAPTER FORTY ONE

Back home I poured myself a nightcap and reviewed the file notes I'd read over at Annie's.

Peter's every move was documented daily, from the moment he woke up to the moment he went to sleep. His places had been bugged, both the house and the Grosvenor Suites. The transcripts of his conversations were all in the file. No stone had been left unturned.

By the time Mike had arrived on the scene Peter's fraudulent scheme was well underway. The files showed many meetings held in and around the Chelsea area. His contingent company bank statements showed the results. He had opened a new bank account for the exercise in the name of B.G.H.L. which he insisted was an acronym for Boerman's Group Holdings Limited. And nobody questioned it. Why would they? Each client knew he worked for Boerman's in a senior investment capacity; even his business cards represented the same information. Meanwhile that account was racking up the funds. By the time he approached Felicity for help in May roughly four hundred million had been accumulated in B.G.H.L.'s name. Not bad for a few months' work. His bank didn't challenge the transactions because he was already a private banking client and therefore, in their eyes, beyond reproach.

Mike Tanner's margin scribbles described his fear that Peter would stop trading before Mike was ready to pounce. But when Peter invited Flick and her family on board Mike knew Waldhan was too greedy to give up this easy route to real wealth. So Mike was waiting to tie them all into the same crime. Until his plan went tits up.

Felicity went off her balcony at home.

But the file was also very helpful in that respect as well. Peter was under round the clock surveillance and there was a section in the report tracking where he went, with whom and when. I smiled ruefully as I read about my own interaction with him. It turned out that when I was following him, I too was being followed out of the gym and back to the

Suites. Similarly there were notes of his visit to my offices and the late night disturbance at my home. But I was fascinated to read how Katey had left my place, quickly followed by him, only for them to meet outside on the steps of my apartment block.

Behaving like close friends apparently.

She'd walked with him back to her place where he'd spent the night.

That was hard to read. After all, I'd done all the warming up. And he'd reaped the reward.

Shame. I thought Katey and I might have had a good thing going.

The file went on to describe the Scotts' new banking arrangements and how they had established a commercial account themselves, one with a surprisingly similar name to B.G.H.L. Only this time it was a limited liability partnership, B.G.H.LLP. Armed with this and some printed business cards and letterheads the Scotts were off and running, going about redesigning Peter's scam in their own name. And very quickly nearly twenty million pounds had accumulated in it from various private names over a few short weeks. It only stopped days prior to Flick's death.

Finally the file documented Peter's movements on that fateful Sunday prior to Flick's death. And it appeared he spent some of it with her and her family.

No action that morning except for the obligatory walk to the newsagents for the Sunday papers. Apparently he was a *Sunday Times/Mail on Sunday* kind of guy. That was the level of report detail. He left again at midday to meet a couple of prospective clients for lunch at Sticks and Sushi where they talked bonds for a couple of hours before he returned home alone. It was mid-afternoon when he made a call to Flick and asked for a meeting between all four of them to clear the air and set the record straight. She was reluctant to entertain him, not trusting his motives, but when he mentioned settling their bonuses she acceded to his request immediately. Early evening and he'd left in a taxi headed for their apartment where he met up with all three of them. But the file made no mention of him leaving their place. None at all.

Mike's large question mark scrawled in the margin next to that section spoke volumes.

I had gone back to the B.G.H.L. and B.G.H.LLP bank statements and no bonus cheques had been presented for payment since that meeting.

I went to bed a couple of hours later knowing two things. I was tired and it was going to take a long cold shower to get me going for the next day. And I was going to have to speak with Heather again and quickly.

CHAPTER FORTY TWO

I was sat in the visitors' meeting area at eleven the next morning feeling like shit and looking the same no doubt. That cold shower idea had been an epic failure. It was supposed to invigorate me for the day ahead. Instead, as I shrunk into the visitors reception area pressed against the wall for comfort in that cold lifeless room, all I felt was tired, miserable, confused and alone.

Last time I was here I was a little too preoccupied with Heather's wellbeing to notice much else around me.

But this time she was late and I took the chance to take in my surroundings as well as some of her cellmates who were also being visited by friends and family. And what a sight they were. Over in the far corner sat a teenage girl with dark bags under her eyes and pale discoloured skin. Her sallow complexion was accentuated by the trademark off white prison overalls hanging loosely from her shrivelled body. She was talking in hushed tones to a bloke sat opposite her who looked totally disinterested in anything she had to say. As I looked on, the chat was getting louder and louder. Soon we could all hear what the problem was.

"But you've got to Leon, I need them now. You don't know what it's like in here. If I don't get them I don't know what'll happen to me."

He murmured something inaudible. She was up in a flash and round to his side of the table, screaming obscenities and flailing her arms all over his head. He managed to cover up from the worst of the blows before the policeman got there and pulled her away, dragging her kicking and screaming abuse all the way down the corridor and back to the cells. You could hear the noise receding as she disappeared from view. Amazingly the rest of the room were wholly unmoved, continuing their private conversations as if nothing had happened. All apart from one solitary woman sat a couple of tables away from me. She was alone, waiting for her visitor and she'd been passing the time staring at me throughout the whole of the previous excitement. She had black, lifeless eyes, piercing and cold. I accidentally got caught in her line of sight and immediately wished I hadn't. She slammed her hands down on the table and growled,

"What the fuck are you looking at?"

Well whatever it was, I stopped looking at it straight away and managed to find a fly to follow on the other side of the room. But her evil malevolent stare was still bearing down on me, making my skin crawl, my nerves jangle. Just when I thought it was probably time to go before I became just another crime statistic, Heather arrived to save the day. I greeted her as a long lost sister, getting up and hugging her tight, like she was my life line to survival. And maybe she was. We sat down and thankfully the psycho looked away, seeking out another victim to terrorise.

"How're you doing today H?"

She didn't need to answer me. It was clear for all to see how she was doing. But she put on a brave face.

"Good thanks. Better than you by the looks of things. What happened? Katey work you over all night and throw you out this morning?"

She smiled weakly. I followed suit, not knowing what else to do. I stroked her hand for want of something more meaningful to do or say. All that was missing were my sympathetic soothing sounds of pity. She looked at me; irritation at what I was doing was written all over her face. I stopped immediately and withdrew my hand by way of apology.

But that left me with no choice but to go to the heart of the matter.

"Heather, I need to ask you some questions about the morning of Flick's death."

No smile this time. Just a hard look of steely determination, her jaws clenched in anger.

"I've told you everything I can about that. I've nothing more to say."

She balled her small hands into tight fists, dragging them to and fro across the table in front of her as if in frustration.

"Okay, so what was Peter Waldhan doing at your home on Sunday evening just hours before it all happened?"

She was stunned by the question. She froze the movement of her fists and looked at me with those deep penetrating eyes. I saw genuine fear, just for a fleeting moment. Then that moment was gone and she leaned back, looking me up and down.

"Who've you been talking to? Where've you got that from?"

I told her about the twenty-four-seven surveillance on Jamie and herself during Mike's three months' controlling influence over investigations into the Boerman's fraud. I omitted to tell her about the phone taps on her place though. She was dealing with enough as it was. When I'd finished, she sighed and her shoulders slumped ever so slightly.

"He asked for a meeting with us to square things off and settle our outstanding financial affairs. We had no choice if we ever wanted to see our bonuses did we? Anyway, that's what happened. He came, he saw and he conquered using nothing more than the power of his cheque book. I don't know what time he left but it was after midnight though. I was tired of it all, so I went to bed and left them drinking in the lounge. The reason I didn't tell you before was we all signed non-disclosure agreements about the whole meeting. To be honest I was just relieved we'd got our money. You do believe me don't you Sam?"

She was lying again and it was happening so often I was beginning to see the signs. Her supplicant tone; her body language; her pleading eyes – they all led to the same place; her disingenuous deceit. I challenged her account of events.

"Those bonuses must have been worth a pretty penny. On my calculations around half a million between the three of you? If you were so anxious about the money, why didn't any of you cash your cheques? I've read the company bank statements and there are no transfers out of the accounts."

She snapped bolt upright and was clearly upset at this line of questioning. I pressed on.

"The Police car surveillance finished abruptly when Flick fell. The officers alerted the emergency services and left their surveillance vehicle outside the building to be in attendance at the scene of the fall. That was at six thirty-five. They have no note of Peter having left the building. According to them Peter didn't leave the premises at all. And by that time, by your own volition, you had stumbled into the grim scenes of violence in your lounge. So was Peter there?"

151

Right there and then I was definitely pushing a point. In fact the Police report stated they couldn't be sure whether Peter had left or not on account of there being several possible ways of exiting the apartment block. And they only had the main one covered. But I reasoned that if she were lying then maybe I could lie a little too.

Whatever my rationale, any remaining colour drained from her face in seconds. She looked visibly shaken by this revelation. Cut to the quick. The silence covered her like a shroud. The atmosphere between us was suddenly thick, acrid, poisonous. But I needed answers.

"If you don't tell me now, I can't help you anymore. My licence may mean nothing to you, but it's all that stands between me and the dole queue. And I'm not over keen on becoming part of the Great Unwashed right now. Truth is, if that were my only problem I might just take the pain of covering for you. Unfortunately for me I'm now so far beyond the Police's definition of what constitutes acceptable detective practice that as well as losing my licence I could easily go to jail myself for perverting the course of justice. And that's not going to happen. So tell me what you're hiding from me, or I'm done with you."

I was bluffing, but she didn't know that. I just hoped I was more convincing than I sounded.

"I can't Sam. I just can't. I'd sooner go to jail for a crime I didn't commit."

She sighed, placed her hands palms down on the table, rested her forehead on the back of them and closed her eyes. But the tears squeezed through anyway. I was talking to the back of her beautiful blonde head.

"Okay then. Okay Heather. That's it. I've got no more."

I stood up, stepped away from the table and out of the visitors' area. I felt her eyes following me as I left the room.

I asked the desk sergeant if I could see Jamie and after a short wait I was back in the visitors' reception room approaching him. He was positioned in exactly the same place as Heather had been. Maybe I'd have better luck with him. He looked very sombre today, his mood was very different so presumably the full enormity of his hopeless situation had finally hit home.

As if to lighten the load I gave him the bric-a-brac he'd asked for the previous day.

I went through the same routine, covering the same issues and got the same basic answers, just in deeper, more gravelly tones. He was giving me the stonewall treatment I'd just suffered at the hands of his sister. He said they'd reconciled their differences with Peter who'd then paid them out and then left sometime after midnight. He couldn't or wouldn't engage in any explanation of the balcony camera footage, except to insist it wasn't him throwing Flick off the building.

I'd had enough and I stood up to leave that place for the second time in half an hour. But he stopped me with a single sweep of his massive hand across the table, grabbing my wrist in his vicelike grip.

"Wait. Have you spoken to Waldhan about this?"

I shook my head.

"You need to."

"Why? The file reports of his police interview confirm your version of events. He says he left about two o'clock and went over to Katey Wilson's for the night. He says he left discreetly using the basement exit. He went back to her place and stayed there until morning. She corroborates his story that he was there with her from around two. What else is there to talk about?"

"Ask him where Katey was earlier that night."

I had no idea what that meant, but he shook his head when I asked him to elaborate.

"I've already said too much. Heather will kill me." His grip loosened, he let go of me and stared down at the floor as he continued. "But he's getting away with murder and there's no one to stop him. Our only hope was the accidental death angle, but Mike Tanner finding those digital images has put paid to that. Gordon Calloway is right; the best we can hope for now is that they can't prove we killed her. And they can't. Because we didn't."

Well at least him and his sister were lying in unison. I said my farewells and left.

On the way back to the office I got a call from Gordon Calloway introducing himself and requesting a meeting, just as Heather had predicted.

"Mr Cove, I've only just come on board but your name keeps cropping up in the interviews I've conducted. I think we should meet, sooner rather than later. Are you available any time today?"

We arranged to see each other in my offices at three. And sure enough here was there at the allotted time. Maggie ushered him into my office, we shook hands and sat down as Maggie served the coffee. When she'd gone a brief moment passed while we both assessed each other. I sipped my coffee and eyed him over my cup.

His carefully manicured shock of silver hair was my first clue to this man's approach to life. He was wearing a sharp three piece woollen suit with grey pinstripes and black brogues. His bright pink shirt touted a wide white collar covering a deep ruby tie that matched his cuff links and handkerchief perfectly. His hands were small and soft to the touch, entirely unused to manual labour of any sort. His highly polished nails emphasised the point. He had an angular face and steel grey eyes that drilled straight through you.

Probably early fifties, but it was hard to tell. What wasn't so hard to work out was that this was a stone cold fish not to be messed around.

I felt pretty confident that his view on meeting me for the first time would not be quite so complimentary. Anyway, it was time to engage.

"So what can I do for you Mr Calloway?"

He crossed his legs as he settled to his work.

"Mr Cove, I've had a look through the charge sheets, the file notes and I've interviewed Jamie and Heather. But there seem to be some missing pieces. And I thought you might help me find them. How well did you know the deceased?"

Two hours, four pots of coffee and reams of copious notes later, Calloway had as much as I could tell him about events as I understood them. He packed his stuff away.

"Now Mr Cove, the one thing you haven't told me is what you think happened here."

That was a heavily loaded question and I couldn't avoid it. I told him of my reservations about the evidence. If Heather and Jamie were on that balcony they must have been there despite knowing they were being filmed. Why? Similarly I described my feelings about lack of motive. If they did kill her, then again, why?

Calloway remained silent while I shared my musings and doubts. When I'd finished he thanked me for my time and stood up to go. But before he left, he had one more piece of news.

"Oh yes. I tried for bail but it was refused on grounds of the serious nature of the charges. That and the fact that Jamie ran from the scene at the time of the death."

That news just reconfirmed my opinion of Jamie as a complete liability. But I couldn't let Calloway leave without having any understanding of his position on the case.

"So what do you think their chances are Gordon?"

"I have no idea at the moment Sam. I need to go away and assemble my thoughts. But those camera images are really quite damning. And the fact that Jamie doesn't want to talk about it doesn't help. If I need to see you again I'll call you. Okay?"

I agreed, we shook hands and he left. It was nearly seven, the street lights were on outside and I was knackered inside. I reached for my mobile and there were three missed calls and a voicemail from Katey. I switched my mobile off.

It was my home time.

CHAPTER FORTY THREE

I slept like a baby. Next morning I was up early and into the office to start my day. I had decided to take Jamie's advice and speak to Peter. But I wondered whether Peter was aware that the police were tracking his movements, or even whether he'd seen that damning balcony film. I called Mike to find out. Sure enough he confirmed that during his police interview Peter had been informed he had been under detailed surveillance. Mike hadn't told him about the terrace footage though. It didn't help Mike's case right now.

I thought we'd finished, but he had something else on his mind.

"Hey Sam, have a good night with my sister? I know Annie did. You read the file notes. Thoughts?"

I told him I'd read the notes. I told him about my meeting with Gordon Calloway the previous day and repeated the reservations I'd expressed about the case. What I didn't do was to tell him about my thoughts on my night out with Annie. Because I didn't want him to know my thoughts about Annie at all. Instead I deflected. "I'm hoping to meet Peter Waldhan later this morning. Anything you want to tell me that might help?" He sounded slightly irritated when he responded.

"It's all in the notes for God's sake. In his interview he was adamant about having left the Scotts sometime before two and Katey Wilson confirms he got round to her place around then. He says he left out of the basement, but Dougie says he was on duty all through the night and never saw Waldhan leave that way. Our problem is that Dougie was caught on the lobby cameras asleep at his desk between one and three that morning. And the fact is those car park cameras are not all functioning properly. I know that to my own cost. So maybe Jamie gave Waldhan a heads up on the best way to leave unnoticed. In any event I can't get behind Waldhan's story at the moment. The whole thing's a mess. The post mortem results don't help much either. They point to the time of death being between five and six thirty. So he was long gone by the time she died according to him. Good luck with Waldhan when you catch up with him."

We said our goodbyes and I hung up.

That left me with trying to get Peter Waldhan to open up about his movements that night.

Suddenly I realised there was very little we had to talk about. He'd done all his talking to the authorities, so why would he grant me an audience to go over the whole sorry incident again? All I had to go on were Jamie's parting words suggesting Katey had a role to play in all this, but I already knew she was at home all night; her police statement confirmed as much.

Unless she was lying.

I was struggling with that dilemma when my mobile rang. It was her.

Maybe I should ask? But I didn't think so… I was still smarting at the police report detailing she'd left me to be with Waldhan that first night he turned up at my apartment and we fought.

No doubt he'd got a sympathy fuck that evening. Yet days later she was fucking my brains out after a Dover Street night to remember.

In any case, if I confronted her she'd probably straight up and lie to me.

Then her lying cheating voice was in my ear.

"Hello stranger. Where've you been all my life? I've called, I've left messages, but no response. I was getting worried about you. Everything okay?"

I didn't have time for small talk this morning. Not with her. In fact I was currently engaged in a wholesale re-evaluation of my relationship with Katey. I didn't know whether she wasn't just another one night stand. A great fuck buddy, but no future.

That didn't help me right now though; she needed a response.

"Everything's good Katey. But it's your unlucky day… I can't talk right now, I've got stuff to do."

"Well fuck you!"

The line went dead. She'd hung up. It must have been something I'd said.

I called Peter and asked how he was.

"Good, thanks Sam. And you?"

"I'm not sure. Can I come and see you?" Another lie. I was absolutely sure how I was feeling; totally pissed off with him and this whole sorry mess. But I had to see him.

"I was with Jamie yesterday and he was in a bit of a state about his circumstances. He's adamant he's innocent of the murder charges and he thinks you know more than you're letting on. Like where Katey was that night you went round to the party. I don't know why he thinks that, so I thought we might talk."

"Well I don't see much point myself, I've already told the police all I know. There's not much more to say."

He was on his hands free and right then I heard Jenny shouting in the background, a torrent of foul mouthed abuse directed at Katey, a rambling rant with no apparent purpose or end. Peter picked up.

"Okay, I'll see you at three."

He put the phone down to stop me hearing her tirade, but I was left hanging, wondering what was going on behind their closed doors right now.

A couple of hours later I jumped into Betty and set off for my meeting. Predictably it was pissing down and Chelsea was literally awash as people with brollies danced along the pavements avoiding the giant puddles where they could. Bit like Gene Kelly in 'Singing in the Rain', but without the accompanying music. And the torrential downpour showed no signs of abating either. Betty aquaplaned to an unceremonious stop right outside the Waldhan residence. And even though I'd parked only a couple of metres from their front door I was still pretty sodden by the time the bells chimed and Peter arrived to pull me inside. He took my coat and we yomped back down to the conservatory. I sat and watched in fascination as the November rain bounced off the glass roof, running down the panes in angry rivulets. Jenny was already there waiting. She looked the model of decorum, totally composed, so different to the febrile animal I'd heard on the other end of the phone only a couple of hours earlier.

"Nice day for it" I said lamely.

They both smiled but said nothing in reply. I looked at Peter.

"I've been to see Heather and Jamie."

Still nothing.

"They've asked me to look into the circumstances behind Flick's death. They say they had nothing to do with it. And Peter, I know you were there the night she died. The police were tailing you. So what happened?"

It was my turn to shut up and listen. For a long time there was no response. Jenny busied herself tracing the raindrops down the window. Peter just looked tired. Finally he spoke up.

"Sam, our relationship with the Scott family is a complicated affair. Apart from Felicity's nanny duties, she was also engaged in a professional capacity with her family selling Boerman's security bonds. And as you know, Jamie and my wife had come to know one another very well on a personal level."

Jenny fidgeted in her chair, adjusting her position so she was cradling her knees against her chest as a defence mechanism.

"I went to their apartment that night to put the record straight. To draw a line under our relationship so we could all move on. And that's what we did. It went on a while, but at the end of it all of our financial and personal ties had been severed – amicably. Then about two I left. Back to Katey's. That's it Sam."

He was looking down at his hands, avoiding any eye contact. Funnily enough Jenny was still staring out of the window, counting rainbows.

"So what do you think happened to Flick?"

I didn't really care what he thought, I just wanted to see how convincing a liar he was.

"When I left the party was in full flow. In particular Jamie was really tying one on. They were all just really happy to have got the whole thing out in the open and, of course, to have their settlement cheques at last. Flick was in great shape. She'd cooked supper and it was a triumph. As for Heather, when I left she'd gone to bed feeling tired. And that was it. I have no idea what happened after that. I walked over to Katey Wilson's and got there sometime after two."

Jenny was now listening intently, bristling at the fact that her husband had gone back to his lover's home that night.

"So there was nothing different about Felicity's behaviour at all?"

He shook his head.

159

"No, nothing. She was her usual cuntish self. Nothing if not consistent. Fucking home wrecker."

I saw Jenny wince.

"And what about you Jenny? Where were you while all this was going on?"

I thought I saw her squirming under the intense pressure of that simple question. There was something very wrong in her demeanour, something simmering underneath that manicured outward composure. And whatever was going on inside that slender frame she was struggling to contain it.

"I've already covered this off with the police. What else is there to say?" she snapped.

She had a point. But so did I.

"Because if you've nothing to hide you should have no problems with the truth. You told the police you were home all night. Didn't you want to know where he was because he certainly wasn't here with you?" I was pointing at Peter.

I was also taking a big chance. Like she said, her statement was clear and unambiguous; she was home all night, unaware of Peter's post-midnight rendezvous. I suppose I was hoping she'd be angry about it all; where Peter was, what he was doing, with whom and for how long. After all, I'd only just been paid for getting rid of Katey as a threat and suddenly it transpired that he was with her the night Flick died. And in all probability giving her the pleasure of his company as well.

But my clumsy attempt at incitement worked. It was as if I'd slapped her hard across the face. She was startled and jumped bolt upright, stung by the memory that Peter had cheated on her.

"That fucking prick."

Her obvious irritation wrapped itself around every syllable as she stared malevolently across at her husband.

"He's just a clueless lying cunt." She was clearly upset.

She pointed her slender finger at him.

"I had no idea he was so angry at me, at my infidelity. Is this his idea of revenge? And now he wants me back he says. Wants a fresh start he says. A move back to Paris and a new life on Ile de Cite he says. Well he'll be fucking lucky unless she's a distant memory, just another messy stain to clean up. Are you going to do that Peter? Clean up your mess? You bastard."

This was not the response I was expecting. She was shaking with rage, so much so that Peter went over to comfort her, but she shrugged him off angrily. They'd obviously got some serious ground to cover yet about love and betrayal.

"I think it's time you left Sam. This whole thing's been very upsetting for Jenny."

I slunk off, confused by Jenny's emotional reaction, but still no wiser and with no more to go on. However, it looked very much as if the Waldhans were making some big new life choices together. I just wondered whether Katey knew.

The rain was still smashing down as I fought Betty's door handle to gain access to her dry worn leather interior. She put up fierce resistance but I had my revenge when she finally let me in because she was instantly wet through too. I was sat there, dripping on the carpets, wondering how the hell I was going to help Heather and Jamie when my mobile rang.

It was Katey again. Fuck. What was wrong with this woman? But this time she sounded desperate.

"What's happening Sam? You seem so distant lately. Is it your work? Is it me? Can I see you? I miss you Sam. Please let me see you. Let's go for a drink or something, let's see each other and talk things through. When can I see you?"

Jesus. What had I done? We'd had a couple of nights' fun together followed by a desperately dreary dinner held in the company of complete strangers. And she'd even been fucking someone else between times. How could that possibly translate into this hysterical, needy cry for help? It was embarrassing. And a bit weird.

For some reason, my thoughts turned to Heather again. Now there was a woman in real need of help. Of support. And it looked like I could do neither. I could feel the anger and frustration building quickly inside, a fire set light by Jenny's irrational outburst before, but now fuelled by Katey's noisy, childish whining for attention. Like the kid who's been pulled past the sweeties by her mother at the checkout, without being allowed to grab a handful.

My idea of hell.

"Stop it Katey. You sound like a spoilt brat. And I've got no time for it. Not now, not ever. Can't you tell I'm busy? Just let me be. I'll call you when I can."

"No! Sam, listen to me. I've made a mistake, a terrible mistake. I need your help!" I shuddered.

"The last time I heard that plea it was from Felicity in my office. I hadn't listened then and look how that turned out.

"I'm serious Sam. I was with Peter the whole of that night. We were at the Scotts' together. I saw it all go down. I witnessed everything. And I'm frightened."

I pushed back on the steering wheel and squeezed it very tight. The air in the car was suddenly cold, heavy, still.

Katey had been there, seen it all. She knew exactly what had happened. I heard a voice in the car. It was mine, whispering.

"Go on."

"The night you and Peter fought I panicked and ran outside. But Peter came out a couple of minutes later while I was waiting for my Uber. He looked a proper state so I took him home and looked after him. He stayed all night."

The way she spoke those words betrayed another truth: they'd slept together that night. And that stung, because I'd put in all the ground work with her that very same night. And he'd taken the prize.

"We spent the whole of the next day together too, which was highly unusual. Normally the weekends were taboo because of Peter's family commitments. But this time we even went to Caprice for a romantic dinner. As far as I was concerned we were back on track. All that night we talked about our future together, a chance to live a life we could never live apart. He stayed again that night but next morning he said he had to go home. He was going to talk to Jenny, explain his feelings for me, work something out with her. He was planning a celebration get-together with the Scotts that Sunday evening. They were signing off on some deals they'd done together and that night was to be pay out night. He invited me over as his guest once they'd finished their business. We agreed that I should be over there at around nine. And that's what I did."

Hmm…I really was going to have to review my pulling technique. I couldn't seem to close the deal with any woman I wanted lately.

"Where are you?" She told me she was at home. "Stay there, I'm on my way."

I parked Betty on the embankment and stepped out into the driving rain. I walked over to the black iron balustrade overlooking the Thames and looked along my beloved river. It was full and angry, swollen by the lashing, horizontal downpour. I could hardly see across to the other side, it was so fierce and insistent. But I put my face to it and looked up at the dark grey clouds scudding past, searching out their next unwitting victims. I wiped my hand across my brow and felt the full, unremitting force of the elements crashing over me. Cleansing my inner soul. I stood there for at least five minutes, collecting my thoughts.

I knew what I had to do now. I went back to the loving arms of Betty and we drove to my place, wrapped in our cold wet embrace.

It was a little after five when I emerged from my shower and I was fully charged by what Katey had said.

I decided Betty had done enough work for one day and I caught a cab over to Fulham. Katey was at the door as I rang the bell.

She'd already anticipated my arrival with her trademark welcoming gin and tonic and it definitely did its job.

I sat down on the sofa but Katey took to prowling the room, scraping her hair back with her hands as she spoke.

"I'm scared Sam, really scared. Peter's a dangerous man to cross and I don't want to upset him."

I could only agree.

"Yes, I know what he's capable of, remember? So what happened when you got to the Scotts'?"

She was shaking as she paced up and down.

"When I walked in the party was in full swing. The kitchen centre island had been turned into a makeshift bar/buffet area, the music was banging out and the small lounge coffee table had several lines of coke ready and waiting. The Scotts were in fine fettle, the drugs and the booze were flowing freely.

"I looked for Peter but he wasn't far away, straddling the back of the sofa, playing air guitar to Dire Straits *Money for Nothing*. They all thought that was hilarious. It was that sort of night. The partying went on and on, drinking games were the order of the evening and we were all slowly drowning in alcohol and cocaine.

"But by four o'clock the mood in the room started to change. Peter was waxing lyrical about his business prowess, his genius in pulling off the perfect fraud against Boerman's. This was all news to me, but by that time I didn't really care what he was going on about; I was too far gone.

"Jamie and Felicity did though. Jamie in particular was getting pretty pissed off about Peter's constant assertions about his skill set and how he'd been let down by his choice of partners. Peter claimed that the whole operation had been torpedoed because of the Scotts' insistence on branching out on their own. Felicity was at pains to point out that there would have been no need for any of that if Peter had honoured his word on the commission payments. Peter countered that he would have done if Jamie hadn't started fucking his wife.

"Heather and I decided to leave everyone to it and sat in the corner giggling at their antics, not realising how deep the feelings went. But by now things were getting ugly. The three of them were on their feet shouting abuse at each other. Tensions were running high. Heather wasn't giggling anymore, she was too busy concentrating on the row brewing over on the other side of the room.

"Suddenly Peter blew up. He was shouting something about Heather and Jamie being lovers. He was recounting a story about the day he found out they'd been having sex with each other. Felicity was understandably distraught. She knew absolutely nothing about any of this and screamed her denials on behalf of the other two. I couldn't believe what I was hearing either. These were two people who'd been good friends to me for years and now Peter was trashing their reputations. But when I turned to Heather, looking for her denials, all I saw was sordid guilt and it was written all over her face. Peter was laughing and mocking, Heather and Jamie were silent and cowed.

"Felicity saw what I saw and she went crazy. It was all happening so quickly; it was like being trapped in a horror movie. Flick grabbed a carving knife from the kitchen and came charging back into the lounge rushing at Peter, screaming and shouting abuse. Peter stood his ground, feet fixed to the floor, waiting, ready. Flick was at him, the knife arcing towards his chest, but he just swivelled her round using her own momentum, then he yanked her back into him, wrapping his arms around her neck. He made it look so easy, almost effortless.

"I still can't believe what happened next. He looked across that room, stared straight at Jamie and with a cold hard smile he snapped her head back on itself and twisted it viciously to the left. We all heard the crack as her neck broke. We watched speechless, horrified as her lifeless body slid off him and onto the carpet in a crumpled heap."

I listened in stunned silence. I was sat very still on the sofa, gripping my drink so tight my knuckles were turning translucent white with the effort. That stuff about Heather and Jamie being lovers was clearly bollocks, Peter was just lashing out in a blind alcohol fuelled rage. But the rest of it was dynamite. I had to get hold of Mike Tanner.

But she hadn't finished yet.

"Jamie reacted first, rushing over to his dead sister hoping she might have survived the assault. But as he knelt over her, he knew she was gone. He looked up at Heather and shook his head. Then he looked over at Peter who seemed entirely disinterested; he just looked back at Jamie and shrugged.

"Jamie snapped. He jumped up and rushed at Peter shouting in anger and frustration. But once again Peter was ready. It took him only a few seconds to dispose of Jamie, leaving him unconscious on the ground. I don't know what he did, but it didn't take long.

"I couldn't move. I was stuck where I was, frozen. Heather went to Felicity's side as Peter turned his attention to her. He told her that if she got the police involved he would out her and Jamie, make their lives impossible, ruin them and their family forever.

"But he seemed to have it all sorted out in his mind. He offered her another option, one where she could save the Scott family reputation while at the same time they would all benefit financially. Peter and I were to dispose of the body over the terrace balustrade and then leave. Heather would tell the police that a great party had gone terribly wrong. The story was to be that Flick and Jamie had fought and she had fallen off the balcony while trying to stab him. Heather was to confirm Peter's attendance at the party 'til two o'clock when he left and went back to Katey's. She was to tell the police that I was never there at all. This was to protect me from getting involved in something that was none of my affair in the first place.

"Believe me, while I didn't really know much about what had been going on between those people, I was more than happy if between them they could contrive a set of circumstances where I was never there.

"The rest of it all happened in a daze. I was numb to it. I'd lost all sense of what I was doing. I just did as I was told. Peter and I went out onto the balcony dragging Flick with us and simply tipped her over the rail. You've got to believe me Sam, all I wanted to do was to get the hell out of there. We ran back to my place using the rear exit, there was too much going on outside the main entrance.

"I was so frightened. I didn't know what to do. I agreed to be Peter's alibi because I thought it would bring us closer together. He said if I helped him we could be together forever. Start a new life, make a fresh start. But he killed her Sam and I'm an accessory. I don't have any feelings for him now, not after what he's done. I can't get past what I witnessed.

"That's why I went to Dover Street with you; to find out if there really was something between us. And to find out if I still had any feelings for Peter. That night in the club I realised I didn't.

"What do I do now Sam? What can I do to make it better?"

I had absolutely no idea.

"There's something you should know Katey. I've just come from Peter's this afternoon. And you shouldn't worry too much about his feelings for you. He and Jenny were planning to leave London. They thought they might be going back to live in Paris together, just one big happy family."

The relief on her face was palpable.

"So you've nothing to worry about there and anyway he's likely going to jail for a long time now. But we've got to get your sworn statement in police hands quickly. I'm going to get Mike Tanner over here."

Thirty minutes later Mike was in Katey's living room, tape recorder at the ready.

When Katey told him she was witness to the whole thing and wanted to revise her statement his face lit up. In fact he nearly fell off his stool.

While she went over her recollection of events the only thing I could hear was his frantic notepad scribbling as he tried to keep up. He didn't need to do it, the recorder would do the job for him. I smiled to myself; he was most definitely old school. I reckoned he'd probably get a kick out of rereading what she was saying in his own words. Throughout the interview he nodded his greater understanding of events he hadn't even been able to work out before. When she finished, he spoke.

"That's it. I'm arresting Peter on suspicion of murder. Well done Katey. You may have taken your time but you've definitely done the right thing.

"Sam, can I have a word?"

He took me out and into the hallway.

"I want you to get over to Charing Cross right now and tell Heather and Jamie what's just happened. Let's see if that loosens their tongues."

He was preaching to the converted. I had a desperate urge to speak with Heather again anyway. I needed to give her a last chance to tell me her truth now I knew Peter was there with Katey that night.

CHAPTER FORTY FOUR

The rain had eased and I took a taxi through the residual London mizzle, across the river and over to the Charing Cross holding centre.

It was outside normal visiting hours but the duty officer seemed to sense my angst. After a couple of minutes pleading my case he went to see what he could do. When he returned he informed me Heather had serious reservations about seeing me at all and Jamie wasn't there, he'd been taken over to Scotland Yard to be interviewed.

But when I walked into that sickly green visitors' reception there she was, trying her best to look pleased I was there with her. She wasn't very convincing.

Her slightly puffy eyes were visible signs of her mood; she'd obviously been in floods of tears recently. We kissed politely and I slid into the bench opposite her. She looked slightly puzzled.

"Why are you here Sam? Last time we spoke I thought it really was the last time. What do you want now?"

"Circumstances have changed Heather. Peter Waldhan has been charged with your sister's murder. He's being interviewed under caution right now. Katey Wilson made another statement about where she was that night. And what she saw. She's confirmed Peter killed Flick. So now you've got to tell me what really happened. I can help. I've got Mike Tanner's ear. He listens to me. If you're innocent of any part in Flick's death, then now's the time to speak up for yourself. It's okay Heather, we know what happened."

I didn't realise but I was squeezing her hands tight in mine, reaching out across that Formica divide between us, looking for a way to help her. She slowly withdrew her hands and held me in her cold level stare.

"Look Sam, I'm tired of all this. We're going round in circles. I've told you before I can't talk about what really happened that night. It's too hard. Too upsetting. I think I'd sooner go to jail and take the rap for

Flick's murder. I don't expect you to understand. I'm not sure I understand myself. But reputations are at stake."

I was angry at her intransigence and at my inability to get through to her what was really at stake.

"For God's sake Heather. You're going to get torn apart. The police have already got enough to lock all three of you up for a very long time. You're all guilty by association. But they won't settle for that. They'll be anxious to get to the bottom of the facts surrounding the murder. There are already gaping holes in the two entirely different versions of events being described by you and your brother. The digital evidence shows the knife being placed in Flick's hand well after she was totally incapacitated. That alone makes you both liars. Katey says you were there all night and you witnessed Flick's death. The Police will think Christmas came early. They'll interrogate you relentlessly, waiting for cracks in your stories to show. And they'll find them no matter how long it takes. Because the cracks are already there.

"Then there's the murder trial. That'll attract major media interest because of Peter's high profile City name and your high profile social media standing. The lawyers will have a field day uncovering all your dirty secrets, whether you like it or not. And have you thought about the court room experience? Have you ever been in a criminal court? It's terrifying if you're the one in the dock. It's bad enough being in the gallery watching. Please don't do this to yourself H. Whatever you're hiding surely can't be worth all that torture? And for what? A twenty-five-year sentence which means twelve years minimum. Your youth, all gone in a moment of madness. And no future on the other side.

"Tell me what you're hiding. Let me help you. Please. Katey says what sparked the row was Peter calling out your incestuous relationship with Jamie. Is that true Heather?"

I couldn't do any more. That was my best shot. I waited for a response and it took some time coming. Heather spent an age pushing some spilt sugar granules round the table top. She seemed fascinated by the new patterns emerging every time she shoved her finger tips between the grains. It was all I could do to stop from screaming. But when she lifted her head it was as if she was lifting a very heavy load with it.

She looked up and sighed in defeat and resignation.

"So Katey's spilt the beans has she? Well good for her. Is what true Sam? Is it true that when Peter accused me and Jamie of fucking each other it caused a fight? Or is it true that I'm in love with my brother? Which one?"

I didn't know any more, but it felt as if something big was coming down the track and I might be in its way. I felt the mood swing in the room and the tension made me feel quite nauseous. I was afraid. She looked straight at me. "Do you love me Sam?

"Sometimes when you look at me I get the feeling you'd do anything for me. Remember that first night at the Pig's when we were sat at the bar? Did you get that spark between us? I did. It was almost scary it was so intense."

I did remember that moment. I remembered it vividly. In fact I'd never forget it.

"Yes, I remember. I still get that feeling whenever I look at you."

I was still smiling at the memory. And the absurdity of our position, declaring feelings we'd never discussed before when we could do absolutely nothing about them now.

"Well that's why Jamie hates you with a passion. He's worried you'll take me away from him. And he needs me more than you can ever know. And I need him too.

"We were never as strong, Jamie and I, never as independent as Flick. After our parents' divorce the three of us became very close, we looked after each other, lived each other's lives in each other's pockets. It was our way of coping. Flick went about getting us work, caring for our financial needs. We simply let her get on with it. And she never let us down. Somehow she got us a slice of our parents' divorce action and that bought us the flat. She got jobs doing all sorts of things to make ends meet. Meanwhile we tried to help out as best we could.

"It was her idea that we start our blog as social influencers. We used her local Facebook contacts and straight away we were on to a good thing. But it was all down to her. And Jamie's good looks of course. The Facebook followers love reading about his playboy lifestyle. And at the same time most of them secretly want to be a part of his seedy world. Little do they know they're the ones paying for it. And he does rather well for female company off those pages. Then he kisses and tells, for the whole world to read. His fans publicly rail against his promiscuity while privately loving to read every juicy morsel about his sleezy goings on. I don't like him behaving like that. In fact it makes me feel sick when I think about it, him sleeping around all over town but as he says, "that's what pays the bills." And that's how he originally met Jenny. She was meant to be just another notch on his bedhead until things got a little more complicated."

Heather had her head down again, talking to the sugar patterns on the greasy table, but I was listening to every word. And feeling distinctly queasy.

"Anyway, when the possibility of selling security bonds presented itself we were only too willing to oblige. And it was so easy. As far as we knew we were simply an adjunct to Peter's fast moving, high flying corporate sales team, giving people high interest safe investments they could rely on way into the future. Truth was it was money for old rope with Boerman's name backing it all.

"Right up until Flick found out it was all fake. The whole thing was a fraud, only on a massive scale. And we couldn't get out of it. In fact we didn't want to get out of it. We found it so all easy to get our social media followers and our Chelsea friends to part with their money. And word was getting out. I was getting more and more enquiries on my blog. Almost too many to handle. The money kept rolling in and when Peter found out and refused to pay us our commissions, Flick decided to do something about it.

"She set up a dummy company and soon we were branching out, going it alone. It was so exciting; for the first time in my life I felt really alive, in control, energised do more and more, make more and more. I didn't care if Peter was bent. None of us did. We only cared about the money we were making. It was like a drug.

"But for Peter it all had to stop. It had gotten out of control. Little did he know about Jamie and Jenny. But he did know about Jamie and me."

She stopped pushing the grains of sugar round the table top and looked up at me. The fresh tears were trickling down her face, the droplets dissolving every sugar grain they came into contact with. Apart from the policeman in the far corner we were the only people in that soulless place and I felt really alone.

What exactly did Peter know about Jamie and Heather that was so devastating in all this mess? I didn't have too long to wait for the answer.

"Do you believe in fate Sam? The idea that we can even attempt to control events around us is an impossible dream in my view. And Jamie and I were just unlucky that day, that's all.

"It was the back end of August and Peter, Jamie and I had just signed off on the biggest bond deal we'd ever negotiated. It was about two million I think and we were on a real high. I remember it like it was yesterday. The ink on the contract was barely dry when the champagne began to flow. We started in the Rivoli Bar at the Ritz which was the ideal place to begin the celebrations. The first bottle of Dom Perignon was downed in minutes, quickly followed by another. By the time, the third bottle was done we'd adjourned to Green Park and snorted our first line of coke for the day. And it was such a perfect day. We sat in the deckchairs and let the summer sun bake us all afternoon, until the coke ran out. Then we wandered over to Trader Vic's at the Hilton and started all over again, this time on cocktails. By seven o'clock we were wasted but we still managed the lift upstairs to the roof top bar.

"However, during the afternoon Peter had been paying me more and more attention. It started with the hugging at the Ritz and his slightly wandering hands. Over in the park the three of us were involved in a lot of horseplay, rolling around in the grass laughing and shouting in our efforts to get at the coke stash. That sort of thing. Peter was constantly bumping into me, grabbing my shoulders, brushing my breasts accidentally, touching my bottom, whatever he thought he could get away with without Jamie noticing.

"But Jamie was noticing.

"He put up with it all day but by the time we were upstairs in the Hilton, Jamie was finished playing gooseberry. He announced he was leaving to find some action. He seemed terribly upset. More upset than I'd ever seen him before. We were all sat overlooking Hyde Park, totalled, spent with all the effort of celebrating our success. Or so I thought. Peter was stroking my thigh and Jamie clearly disapproved. Suddenly he got up to go. 'Jesus Heather. Why don't you two just get a room?' And with that he stormed out. I rushed after him and caught him at the lift.

"'Jamie, what's wrong?'

"But I already knew what was wrong. In fact I'd been playing up to it all day. I'd felt the thrill of his jealous eyes. I'd seen the furious passion burning in them. And the fact that I felt the same way was not lost on him either. It was the unspoken tryst between us. The dark secret that could never be shared or spoken. He was really wound up. I'd pushed it too far,

"I knew he was angry and I wanted to apologise. So I kissed him. It was only intended as a soft reminder of our secret feelings, what was and was not possible. But he grabbed me in his arms and crushed me to him, kissing me all over my face and neck. I don't know why, but in that moment my feelings overwhelmed me. I grabbed him back, crashing him up against the elevator door, sliding and rolling us both along it in our frenzied embrace, kissing him hard, feverishly. I can still remember the taste of him on my mouth, his hands seeking me inside my pants. And the wetness that was already there to greet him. We'd gone far too far but he'd probably have thrown me on the carpet and done me there and then if Peter hadn't interrupted us. He'd come out of the bar to see what was wrong and stumbled into us mauling one another. We rolled away from each other but it was too late; he'd seen everything he needed to see.

"I'll never forget that moment. Nothing was said. The three of us just stood in silence trying to take in what had just happened. Then the lift came, the doors opened and Peter went downstairs without saying a word. But that ugly crooked smile on his face as the lift doors closed will stay with me for the rest of my life.

"I was devastated. It was all I could do to get home; I wouldn't have managed it without Jamie's help. Our secret was out. The unspoken secret of our lifetime. And even though we'd first had sex when I was twelve and he was fifteen, nevertheless it felt like we made love for the first time that night back at the apartment.

"And that's the truth Sam. The truth about me and Jamie."

CHAPTER FORTY FIVE

Not for the first time since I'd known the Scotts, I was speechless. There were no words to express what I was feeling.

I didn't trust myself to look her in the face. I was gutted. And incensed. And distraught. All at once. As I thought about him putting his hands on her perfect body I felt physically sick, wretched, appalled.

But more than anything else I felt loss. My loss.

Like when I finally realised my wife was gone from me, the love of my life, all because of a drunken, drug fuelled moment of weakness with her friend.

But it was more than that. I'd only known Heather a short time yet I'd thought there was something special between us, some bond forged in her adversity. And somewhere in me there was an overwhelming desire to keep her safe from harm.

The anger came from nowhere, sweeping through my body, that white hot burning fire coursing through my very being, threatening to consume my soul.

I remembered that first night at the Pig's when I saw her leave with him, the both of them locked in each other's embrace. Him casually wandering around their flat, semi naked. Their stolen looks of intimacy over breakfast at Joe & the Juice's.

I'd simply ignored the signs. What a fool I'd been.

I winced at the effort it took to bring myself back under control. And it was as if she felt my pain. Her hand slid over mine.

"I'm sorry Sam. It was never meant to be this way. But we can't help ourselves. Of course Mum and Dad never knew. That knowledge would have been far too much for their fragile marriage to bear. As it goes the marriage eventually collapsed under its own weight, it had nothing to do with Jamie and me. But they still don't know. It'd kill them if they found out, even now. As for Felicity, well she just loved us both for what we were and couldn't see past that. She had no idea what was going on, or if she did she hid it remarkably well. There were no recriminations, no anger, no discussion. Just her pure unadulterated love for two people she cared deeply for."

Heather snapped herself out of her own private thoughts and her knuckles tightened over mine. She didn't know it but her touch was making me feel physically sick. I withdrew my hand.

"But Peter? Well there's a whole other kettle of fish. The old relationship between us and him was suddenly as nothing. He turned mean, distant. Nothing we could do was good enough for him anymore. We were still pulling in the contracts and the bank balance was getting bigger every day. But the contact between us was gone. The intimacy of shared success, those casual mid-week drinks, the shockingly inappropriate e-mails, everything. All that was left was the isolation of Jamie, Flick and me, all of us cut loose and operating in a vacuum.

"But it was when the commission cheques stopped that we knew something was really wrong. We confronted Peter and he told us the deal had changed. He was under pressure from Boerman's to reduce his deal margins he said. He couldn't afford us anymore he said. It was about that time Flick's friend told us about his fraudulent activity and we realised we'd been duped. Yet still he flatly refused to pay us our commissions. And it was a lot of money. So we set up our own arrangements using Boerman's as a front, just like he had. Flick arranged it all, the bank account, the letterheads and office back up, the business cards, everything. It was that simple.

"And it went well. Better than we could have ever imagined in fact. Right up until Peter found out what we were up to. He called a meeting at his house and when we got there he went berserk. Because it was the same day Jenny spilled the beans about her and Jamie."

Heather was staring out of those skylight bars, looking wistfully up at that narrow window to freedom.

But all I could see was a wall of blackness, bleak hopeless dark, stretching out in front of me all the way to my horizon. I felt betrayed, cheated out of what might have been even though Heather and I never really had a chance. She didn't care about me; she was locked in her own depraved immoral world where somehow she'd become the victim of

Peter Waldhan's recriminations when he too found he couldn't have her. It was tough to bear, but I persevered.

"He was so angry. He threatened to crash the whole operation and throw himself on Boerman's mercy by sacrificing the three of us up to the Police. We left, frightened and worried that he would follow through. When he called that Sunday to arrange a settlement meeting we were all so relieved. There was a lot of pain going round and we all felt it was time to draw a line under past events.

"But what happened that night went beyond the pale. Jamie and I decided we could never speak of it again. It was all too grotesque. But now your new lover has told the whole world about my tawdry incestuous affair. Except it isn't tawdry. We love one another. We always have. We always will."

She fixed me with her crystal blue stare and a single tear slowly formed in the corner of her eye, skipped down her weary face and into the sugary puddle below.

I suddenly felt incredibly tired. Tired and weary of the whole thing. My body was numb with the revelations; processing it all was a bigger job than I could possibly handle. I stood up.

"Goodbye H."

I turned and walked away, wiping my own tears with my sleeve, like a small child who's lost his Mum and fears he might never find her again.

Or the man who's just had his lifetime's dreams crushed by a reality so devastating he can never get past it.

CHAPTER FORTY SIX

The walk back to the Yard was a slow, solitary affair. I let the winter rain mingle with my tears in a vain attempt to wash the pain away. Mike had said he'd be there after I'd seen Heather, so I had to give him a heads up.

He needed to know about Heather's involvement in the fraud. But he didn't need to know it from a gibbering broken wreck of a man stumbling along Whitehall, gulping back the tears.

He'd be interviewing Heather pretty soon now and her private words to me might make a difference.

I decided not to tell Mike about Heather and Jamie's incest. I didn't see the relevance. Somehow I needed to put aside her confessions of love for Jamie. Anyway I didn't know how they materially affected the murder charges, if at all.

But she had just confessed that her family fraudulently misrepresented themselves as Boerman's agents then sold completely unsecured bonds to a whole bunch of trusting friends in west London and environs.

What she hadn't done, consistently refused to do, was to admit she killed her sister, or even talk about it. And as I recalled the way she spoke about her sister in that visitors' reception room, she never would. Jamie had been just as convincing when he talked about Flick's final moments.

And now I knew why. They were trying to cover up their own ugly illicit relationship. Their sordid, dirty little secret.

I walked by that Guardsman again. He was still standing implacably to attention, rivulets of rain running freely off his busby, right down his bright red tunic, splashing onto his mirror black shiny boots. His rifle stood to attention with him, bayonet fixed, ready for battle, or anything else bothering the Queen on that grey, miserable wet evening. I was in the mood to take a good old stabbing myself right now, but I just smiled and nodded as I passed by.

Then I was back inside Scotland Yard and a couple of minutes after that I was in Mike's office.

He sat me down and we talked about Heather's criminal relationship with Jamie and Flick. Or at least I did. About five minutes in to my review Mike sensed something was wrong with me. He went over to the drinks cabinet hidden in the corner and poured us both a huge slug of Johnny Walker Blue label. I drank mine in one and he went back and got the bottle. I wanted to tell Mike what had just happened to me. What Heather had told me about her and her brother. But I just couldn't. It was too painful. At one point I thought I might break down, shielding my face from the blame associated with crying in public. That was another thing drilled into me at an early age. But Mike's expensive private education meant he too understood when a stiff upper lip was required and when you could let your guard down, just for a moment. So he got my embarrassment even though he didn't know why and he allowed me the space to cry… just for a short time. I swallowed the urge to spit out my bitter diatribe, to rail against the bad luck that pitted me against the most primeval forces of nature; sibling love. A love that had found me so incapable of understanding its depth. Eventually my inner madness subsided.

"So what happens now Chief Inspector Tanner? What's your approach to be?"

I wiped my eyes again, a habit I was slipping into far too frequently nowadays.

"I get Heather in here for questioning right now and we nail her on the conspiracy to defraud. Meanwhile I go see Jamie and see how he likes the idea of joining her in jail for twenty to thirty years for the same thing.

As for the murder, it's time to confront Waldhan with Katey's truth."

CHAPTER FORTY SEVEN

I was dispatched back to the small room with the two-way glass and watched on as the two interrogating officers were replaced by Mike and a colleague. The whole interview process was restarted. The audio in my room wasn't great, but it was good enough for me to follow events. Mike kicked things off with his tape recording.

"The time is seven ten p.m. Present in the room are Mr James Scott, his solicitor Mr Gordon Calloway, Detective Inspector Malcolm Price and Detective Chief Inspector Michael Tanner. Interview begins."

Jamie looked completely shot. He'd been in there nearly nine hours, nine hours of constant questioning, constant inquisition and constant reinvestigation of his story. He needed a good old shower and a shave to lift his spirits. Sadly neither were on offer. Calloway too had seen better days. He'd been scribbling away for the same length of time; he had two full notebooks and a recorder with three spent tapes next to him as if to prove the point. Meanwhile Mike and Malcolm were each sat eating a sandwich with a cup of coffee for comfort. No such luxuries for the other two. I didn't fancy being Jamie today.

He didn't know about Katey's changed statement. And his inquisitors did.

Mike spoke directly to him.

"Mr Scott. I'd like to turn to the events on the evening of twenty third November at your apartment. You've already stated you received a call from Peter Waldhan that afternoon seeking a meeting with you. Tell me what happened when he got there."

Mike was staring at Jamie who was curiously preoccupied with the laces on his sneakers.

Jamie looked up.

"No."

Katey's damning evidence was going to bite him in the bollocks right about now.

Mike ignored the response.

"Mr Scott, do you know Ms Katey Wilson?"

Jamie's head snapped up and he stared straight at Mike, slightly confused.

"Yes I know Ms Katey Wilson. She's a family friend. Why?"

He was looking hesitant now, unsure of what was coming next.

"Because we've just finished taking her revised statement of events that evening and it's very illuminating. She saw everything and she's willing to swear to what she saw. Now will you tell me what happened that night?"

I wasn't a keen fan of Jamie's. For me he was the epitome of what happens when donkeys and orangutans go on a date. But right now he was doing a pretty decent impression of a guppy in a fish bowl, mouth opening and closing but no words forthcoming. He was pale with fear as he came to terms with what he'd just heard. Finally he gathered his senses and spoke.

"And what's she got to say for herself?"

Mike read back Katey's new statement while Jamie sat still, dumbfounded. He didn't mention the part about Peter forcing Jamie's relationship with Heather out into the open. He didn't need to. Anyway, as far as Mike knew it was just rumour, hearsay. I knew it was so much more than that, but I hadn't told Mike about it because it wasn't necessary. Anyway, I wasn't strong enough.

Jamie looked on in fascination as Mike walked him through Katey's testimony. When Mike finished, Jamie could contain himself no longer.

"Well I'm glad that fucking bitch has let it all out. I was never in favour of Peter's idea; like most of his initiatives it was doomed to failure and I had no desire to see my life out in jail for a crime I didn't commit. I only did it for Heather."

Those last six words summed up most of my recent life, ever since I'd met her.

Jamie spilled his guts, confirming everything Katey had said. He went back to Charing Cross and prepared for freedom. And a showdown with Heather.

Peter Waldhan was a lost cause now.

CHAPTER FORTY EIGHT

Mike ushered me across the corridor and into another small room with two-way glass. He had a childish spring in his step. He was so happy I thought he might start skipping and playing hopscotch.

"I love it when a plan comes together. You've been instrumental in all this Sam; I owe you one. Now I wonder what Mr Waldhan will have to say for himself when he hears about Katey's change of heart?"

I didn't wonder. It didn't matter much what Peter Waldhan said. He was well and truly fucked.

What Mike really meant was that he was going to enjoy watching Waldhan's face as the final truth of his guilt hit him. I have to confess, I was looking forward to that moment too.

Mike left me alone to go and engage Peter on the other side of the glass.

Five minutes later Waldhan appeared in my eyeline accompanied by his Brief, a striking blonde touting a black two-piece suit, a white shirt and black heels. I'd give him one thing, this man knew how to surround himself with striking women.

They sat across from Mike and the intrepid Malcolm Price who, as I far as could recall, hadn't said a word throughout the whole interview proceedings. Maybe he was Mike's lucky mascot. Maybe he was Mike's bit on the side; I was so confused nowadays.

Mike started the interview and went straight for the jugular.

"Mr Waldhan, we re-interviewed Katey Wilson this afternoon at her request. And she's now saying she was at the party all night; saw everything; saw you kill Felicity Scott then helped you dump her body over the terrace balustrade. She also says you coerced her into providing you with an alibi by promising to take her away, be with her as her partner. What have you to say to all of that?"

Mike leaned back in his chair locking his hands behind his head and waited for Waldhan's response. I was sat forward on mine, eagerly waiting for the same thing.

Waldhan was motionless. Steely eyed. Completely unmoved. What was that man made of?

His leggy blonde Brief leaned over and whispered in his ear, but he shook his head and disengaged. He leaned back in his seat as well, balancing it on two legs pushing his hands deep down into his pockets, almost stabilising himself for what was to come.

"She did, did she? How is the old girl?"

He paused as if to collect his thoughts, then he continued.

"I remember the night we first met. I was drowning my sorrows in the Pig's. She was a friend of Felicity's... everyone was a friend of Felicity's. I bumped into her on my way to the toilet and she was still waiting for me when I came out. Nothing if not pushy that woman."

He was in some place far away from that interview room. A place where no one else could go unless he took them there. He was recounting his time with Katey like he had nothing better to do. Like he was telling a casual story in a bar full of strangers.

I was gradually moving closer and closer to the glass, frightened in case I missed something.

"I think I fell in love with her that moment. I can't be sure because I was still trying to get over the fact that my wife was fucking Jamie Scott, but I think it was then.

"She was so fresh and innocent, so desperate to be a part of something bigger than what she had. A real socialite climber. And I could help her there. Anyway, I have no regrets about Katey. I would have taken her away with me if this hadn't happened. Felicity ruined my marriage; I could never be with Jenny again, not after Jamie had soiled her.

"I invited Katey to be with me that night at the Scotts' because I wanted us to celebrate together. It was meant to be a new start for us all, the Scotts, me and Katey. But it just didn't work out like that. It's worth noting that Katey had no knowledge of what we were all up to, she was just an innocent bystander. I just wanted her to be a part of the celebrations. I thought she and I had a lot to celebrate and we had a lot more to look forward to as a couple. But it wasn't to be.

"There was too much bad energy at the Scotts'; the booze and drugs just fuelled those flames of anger and distrust that night.

"I didn't go there to kill Felicity. But she deserved it after what she'd done to my life. I have no regrets about her death. My only regret is that Katey and I will never get to live our dream."

He signed his confession an hour later.

CHAPTER FORTY NINE

I caught a taxi back to my place and my thoughts turned to Betty because we both had a lot to think about. She was working out how to persuade me to replace her rusted running boards. I was working out how to repair my shattered emotions.

And the day wasn't over yet. I still owed Katey a call to see how she was. And to finish things.

I called her when I got home and asked her out for a drink at the Pig's. It somehow seemed an appropriate venue to say goodbye.

I got there at nine o'clock as agreed and this time she was already there sat in a cosy booth well away from the dance floor action, cradling my Long Island for me. I sat down reaching for my drink but she pulled it away.

"You can't have it yet, not before I get my own personal welcome."

Even in that dim light I could see she'd been drinking.

She leaned over and forced her lips on mine, urgently seeking the passion we'd both shown each other just a few nights earlier. It was awful. Desperate stuff.

I pulled away in embarrassment yet still managing a false smile of greeting.

"Hi Katey. How are you doing? I know you told Mike everything he needed, but it couldn't have been easy. And Peter's confessed on the back of your statement. You okay?"

I reached for my drink again and this time she granted me access. The first swig was to settle my nerves, the second to take away the taste of her lips.

We could never be as we once might have been, not now I knew how her childlike mind worked. Not now I knew she'd witnessed Peter kill Flick then cover for the killer.

She leaned across to me and I could smell the gin on her breath.

"It was a nightmare. I don't know whether they're going to press charges as an accessory, but I don't think Mike Tanner's heart is in it. He was more concerned with getting to the truth of what really happened to Flick. I suppose Peter's in a lot of trouble isn't he?"

I looked at her and saw her in a new light.

A small child, struggling to find her way in a world where she had no influence apart from her looks and her contacts. Like so many in her Chelsea set.

"Yes he is."

I suddenly needed to go, to get away from her and everything she stood for. She made me feel uncomfortable, dirty. Unfortunately, she didn't see things the same way.

"So what about us Sam? Do you think we can make a go of it now this is all over? You know I want to try don't you?"

She was sliding across the seat, moving closer, too close.

I gulped my drink in one and stood up.

"No I don't think so Katey. You're a bit too much woman for a simple man like me."

I walked out of the Pig's feeling pretty good about myself for the first time in a very long time.

CHAPTER FIFTY

Next morning and visiting hours found me standing in the queue outside Charing Cross Police station again, waiting to see Heather. But this time I was there to pick her and Jamie up.

When they appeared I was looking at two very different people. She looked much more like the old Heather I knew and loved. She was wearing her own clothes again and even though she was only wearing a shirt and jeans with a fur jacket, she looked fantastic. As for Jamie, he'd spent enough time in front of his prison mirror to ensure that he would still be the pin up boy of the blogging fraternity.

I introduced them to Betty and when Jamie had stopped laughing I drove them back to our apartment block with him crammed in the back.

Heather invited me up for a coffee, but Jamie had to go. He had some catching up to do. I could only assume he'd arranged some sexual welcome elsewhere.

But when he'd gone, I sensed a change of mood.

We sat down with our coffees and Heather wanted to talk, to explain her version of events the night Flick had been killed. She said it would be cathartic, and certainly it seemed to me we could both benefit from a dose of the truth.

So I was all ears.

"Peter came round that night. And he came alone. But Katey joined him a couple of hours later. She'd come in through the carpark entrance like she usually did. Flick had given her the key codes to get in a long time before.

"It was all very civilised at first. We drank, we ate and we all laughed together, enjoying each other's company for one last time. But it all went on far too long, the drink and the drugs were flowing fast and free.

"Waldhan wrote out our cheques and in return we transferred the twenty million into his account electronically there and then.

"But after a while he started waxing lyrical about his brilliance, his ability to pull off the perfect scam, all of it brought down because of our family greed and avarice. It was the drink talking of course, but a row erupted and the booze addled insults flew to and fro. Jamie in particular was on the warpath, insisting it was Peter who was the man consumed by greed, to the point where he'd pushed us too far by denying us our hard earned bonus payments.

"Peter countered with the fact that Flick had set up in competition and as a result twenty million pounds had gone missing into the Scotts' separate company account.

"The arguments went on and on, getting louder and louder. It was nearly daylight and Peter and Jamie were high on neat whisky by this time. Both were on their feet stalking the room, circling one another.

"Then Peter made a terrible mistake.

"He brought up the issue of Jamie and me and our little secret. He told Flick about what had happened that day at the Ritz and after. He left nothing out, nothing to the imagination.

"Flick was simply stunned at his outburst. Shocked and furious in equal measure that such an allegation should be brought on her own flesh and blood. Even the possibility that we could be like that with one another was complete anathema. She let rip, screaming insults, shouting her disbelief, appalled that Peter could even suggest such a thing was happening under her very own roof.

"Eventually her ranting began to subside and she looked across at Jamie and me, seeking support and a total denial from us. But we couldn't do it. The timing could have been better, but she had a right to know the truth about her own brother and sister.

"She didn't get it at first, refusing to accept what our silence represented. But as this new reality sank in she was pretty shaken up. She even had some trouble breathing, shaking her head in disbelief. It was all very dramatic, all very Flick. She started screaming and ran over to the kitchen drawer. She pulled out a carving knife and came rushing back into the lounge targeting all her anger and abuse at Peter. She lunged at him, screaming and bawling her indignation and shame. It all happened so fast. He was facing her square on; he grabbed her wrist and whipped her round, all in one motion. Before we knew what was happening he had his arms wrapped round her neck and we heard the snap as he twisted her head back across his body in one sharp movement of his arms and hands. It all seemed so effortless for him; it seemed to happen in slow motion; she just slid out of his arms and onto the floor. The sickening crack that was her neck breaking was such a horrible sound, so deliberate, so final.

"And all Peter could do was smile as he let her fall. It was as if he'd been waiting for this moment all his life.

"Jamie was first to react, I was frozen where I sat. He rushed over to her, falling to his knees by her side. He attempted triage but there was no discernible response. Finally he looked up at me and shook his head. Then he looked across at Peter and he was angry, furious, out of control. I'd seen that look before so I knew exactly what was going to happen next.

"Jamie stood up slowly, deliberately. He didn't take his eyes off Peter as he stepped over Flick's body towards him.

"Peter was ready though. He didn't care if Jamie was bigger and stronger. He bounced into position and adopted that karate defence stance. But Jamie didn't care about any of that. He picked up the knife and rushed Waldhan. They both hit the ground rolling over and over. The furniture went everywhere. Peter got back up first and kicked Jamie full in the face at point blank range. While Jamie was reeling from the force of that blow he hit him again, this time with the heel of his hand, so hard Jamie's eye closed almost instantly. Jamie wasn't finished yet though and he came back for more. He walked right into another bone shaker of a punch aimed right between his eyes. This time Jamie went down on his knees. He tried to clear his head but Peter had other ideas. He stood over Jamie, then he kicked him in the side of his head so hard you could hear it over where I was across the other side of the room. And that was it. Jamie slumped to the floor, out cold.

"And all the time Katey was looking on, watching what was happening, frightened out of her wits. I ran over to my brother, my lover, to see if he was still breathing and thank God he was. I turned to Peter and Katey."

Just about now Heather was reliving every word, every moment of that terrible morning as if we were both there too.

"'What have you done?' 'You've killed my Flick.'

"I was in a state of shock, traumatised by the cold carnage I'd just witnessed. But Peter wasn't finished yet. He carried a threat meant just for me. He had it all worked out. He said if I told anyone about what had happened I'd regret it for the rest of my life. He said he'd expose Jamie and me as lovers. He'd tell my family and the whole world. He said he'd go to prison for murder but he'd make sure my personal life was finished. He'd tell the Press and the rest of the media pack. He said he'd make sure they haunted me and Jamie for the rest of our lives.

"Then he suggested another way to go. One where we could keep our reputations and our money.

"He said he and Katey would dispose of Flick's body over the balcony. Me and Jamie would make out to the police the whole thing was the result of a horrible family feud gone wrong. We'd tell them Jamie and Flick had a massive row about his relationship with Jenny and then Flick stabbed him. He even went over to Jamie's prostrate body and slashed his arm with the knife so the police would think Flick had done it. We were to say Jamie had run out on to the terrace to escape her but she was totally out of control. She had run after him, where in a desperate lunge she missed him and went straight over the balcony and plunged down to her death.

"He said we should tell the police he was here alone and left to go back to Katey's around two. And Katey was never here at all.

"He said he'd reissue the bonus payments and reallocate Flick's share to the two of us once the dust had settled.

"And then Katey and Peter just dragged Flick through the patio door and threw her over the balcony rail. I couldn't believe what I was witnessing.

"Then they were gone. Like ghosts in the night.

"I looked over and Jamie was bleeding so badly I ran to the bathroom for some water and towels. When I returned he was sitting up holding his head, looking confused. I cleaned him up and told him what had just happened, what Peter wanted us to do, what our story was to be and what the consequences would be if we didn't do exactly as he said.

"Jamie couldn't get his head round it at first. But we both realised we had to do something and fast. We ran outside and saw Flick's contorted body nine storeys below. A crowd was starting to gather. We rushed back inside and I called the police and we tied our story together as best we could while Jamie was packing.

"We rationalised that Flick was dead and nothing could bring her back. She shouldn't have attacked Peter with a knife and the fact that she'd done that was because of what we'd done, nothing to do with Peter Waldhan at all. He'd acted in self-defence, that's all. And we might as well make the best of it. At least doing it Peter's way we could protect the family name from harm and keep the money we'd worked so hard to make. All we had to do was to forget his malevolent smile when he snapped Felicity's neck.

"It was Jamie's idea to run away. He thought that he would be a distraction for the police, keep them preoccupied, turning their attention away from me.

"So we said our goodbyes and kissed. Then he left taking the Mercedes with him out the back way through the basement car park.

"And I was left to face the police alone."

She stood up and looked down on my stunned expression of horror and disbelief. She put her fingertips to her lips then placed them softly against mine.

"You deserved better than this Sam. I wish things hadn't turned out this way. But I think you should go now."

So did I. And the sooner the better. I did as I was told.

CHAPTER FIFTY ONE

Back in my office I was busy licking my wounds, feeling incredibly sorry for myself. Cosying up to my old mate Jack.

You could always trust Jack. Jack was like a faithful old dog. He just wanted to be with you, to share your life, to make everything easier for you. You wouldn't find him recreating history just so he could cash in on his murdered sister's life. Or regularly fucking his other sister either.

I decided I wasn't cut out for a career as a private investigator. I was definitely in the wrong profession.

Mid-afternoon I got a surprise call from Annie inviting me over for drinks that night. Mike was going to be there too, which was good news for me; he had a lot of explaining to do.

I arrived at eight and Annie was there to greet me, looking absolutely radiant, stunningly but casually gorgeous. And she managed all that dressed only in hipster jeans, tight white vest and bare feet. All the beautiful people could pull that look off without even trying. Me? Well I relied heavily on my clothes and hair to do that work, and it almost always failed. I usually ended up looking like something the cat dragged in. And tonight was no exception.

She ushered me into her reception room and we sat across from one another soaking in the warmth of the fire, the cosy table lamps throwing their low yellow light all around the room. It all felt very welcoming as Mike walked in, drinks tray in hands.

"Hello, Sam. We thought we'd ask you round to celebrate the outcome of Flick's case."

He set the tray down and poured the Courvoisier into three champagne flutes, followed by the Dom Perignon filled to the rim. As he passed the glasses around, he made a point of commenting on my dress sense.

"I hope you're not expecting food too, I broke the bank getting the drinks sorted!"

How could I be overdressed wearing chinos and a Lauren sweater I wondered. Still that champagne cocktail was an absolute delight. And it was over too soon as I looked down at an empty glass. Fortunately, Mike was on hand with a refill.

I thanked him and waited to hear all the news about the rest of the day's events. Presumably, that's why I'd been invited round. But in the end he needed prompting, he was paying the cocktails far too much attention.

"Well Mike? How did you get on today? Any more skeletons fall out of the Scotts' dark, desperate cupboard?"

I wasn't particularly interested in his answer. Frankly, I was struggling to take my eyes off Annie's perfectly formed feet and ankles. And anything else I could sneak a peek at when she wasn't looking. Because she wasn't wearing a bra. But Mike was talking and I was soon paying attention.

"That Katey Wilson's a piece of work isn't she? She wasn't sure which of you was the best bet, so she played you both! Sorry Sam, I know you and her had a bit of a thing going, but you couldn't possibly have known quite how duplicitous she was.

"Waldhan was easy meat after he heard about Katey's change of heart. He really loves that woman, not that it's going to do him much good now, eh? He confessed to killing Felicity but claims it was an act of self-defence. Well we'll just see about that. His lawyer's argument will be tested in court.

"Jenny Waldhan's suing for divorce; I don't know what grounds she'll go for, but she's spoilt for choice isn't she?

"As for Heather, she confessed to her part in the Boerman's fraud, implicating Jamie in it as well. She was more concerned about what her loyal fans would say about her incestuous relationship with her brother when it all came out in court. But she seemed resigned to the fact that she'd been outed… almost relieved after all that time living a monstrous lie.

"Sorry about that too Sam. Seems like you've just got unlucky with your women this time out. But you really shouldn't make a habit of it; after all you've got your reputation to think of…

"Jamie felt the same way as his sister, just thankful it was all out in the open. He was more worried about the effect on his sex life without his loyal female followers trailing behind him anymore.

"Oddly enough neither of them were worried about doing time, as long as they did it together."

I'd been listening and drinking in equal measure while Mike spoke, with Annie topping me up along the way. By the time he was done I was finishing my third cocktail and looking to Annie for another. I was reminded how I felt that day with Peter Waldhan, drinking brandy at the Grosvenor Suites. If only I'd known who I was drinking with.

But there was something else I needed to know.

"I've got a question for you Mike. Why didn't you keep me in the loop? There've been three or four occasions over the past couple of weeks when you've had information that might have helped me to help you. Like your prior knowledge about that camera footage. Or the fact that you already knew Waldhan was at Katey's flat on the morning of the murder. Even the first time we met you forgot to tell me you'd already visited the scene of the crime. And yet you let me see the file notes that night when I brought Annie home. What was all that about?"

I simply didn't understand. But Annie did. She giggled in her charming girly way, hiding her mouth behind her hands like she was doing something naughty. She busied herself by fixing me another drink. Mike was smiling too.

"That's easy. I needed to know."

Needed to know what? Annie was getting giddy now, almost bouncing up and down on the edge of her armchair waiting for his explanation.

"I've been in C.I.D. for ten years or more. And it can be an incredibly frustrating experience. As an active law enforcer the hurdles you have to jump to turn an arrest into a conviction are quite formidable.

"And the biggest one is the red tape that surrounds every action you take. Every interview; all that political correctness; all those people intent on stopping you doing your job. I've had to deal with it all my Police life, but lately it's getting worse. It's like I'm treading on eggshells trying to find the truth amidst the piles of administrative and politically correct bullshit.

"In short, I need help. I need someone who isn't bound by Police protocol and bureaucracy. Someone who operates outside the operational guidelines that inevitably inhibit solid Police work. Someone like you.

"So I had to find out how good you are when left to your own devices. And you passed the test with flying colours. You eventually got behind the Scotts' elaborate façade of respectability; exposed the duplicity of the Peter Waldhan's miscreant lifestyle.

"In short you got to places I couldn't or wasn't allowed to go. It was only when you got stuck I felt the need to try and help you. And that wasn't really necessary, was it?

"So I've got a proposition for you. Going forward I want to use your somewhat unusual skill set to help me do my job. You'll be a secret member of my team, contracted as a sort of private Police investigator. Using your offices as cover for my more unorthodox crime prevention. You'll be undercover and if ever found out I will deny any knowledge of your existence… you'll be all on your own.

"But by working closely together I think we can make a difference to the way the Police get to the truth and catch the bad people. And I'm authorised to offer you two hundred grand a year plus expenses for your services. What do you think?"

I sat back wide eyed and took a good old slug of my heavily laced champagne cocktail. Looking over at Annie I could see the glint of excitement in her eyes. And she was right, it was an exciting prospect.

The idea that I might be able to go about my affairs with a client base on tap and back up resources unimaginable on my own was really quite appealing.

But so was working alone, responsible to no one but myself; the ability to move in the shadows; do my own thing, in my own way. That was deeply ingrained in me too.

I shuffled in my seat, keenly conscious of the two sets of eyes watching my every move. I was suddenly acutely aware of the growing, insistent silence which hung heavy over the room.

"I don't know what to say. I really don't. I've never considered any other m.o. for doing what I do. My job suits my lifestyle just like it is. Largely unencumbered by those many strictures you've just described.

Me, on my own, with no one else to answer to. I don't know Mike, I really don't."

Both Mike and Annie looked crestfallen, surprised at my reluctance, my stiff cold response.

"Is it the money? Is that the issue? Because if it is, we can talk about that. I have some latitude."

He didn't understand. Well that was okay, I'm not even sure I did. But I did know it had nothing to do with money.

"Let me go away and think about it. Now who's for another drink?"

CHAPTER FIFTY TWO

Flick's funeral was a desperately sad affair.

It seemed most of the Scotts' blogging fraternity had shown up to say goodbye, all chanting and yelling their good wishes from beyond the church gates.

Heather and Jamie led the procession and as I watched fifty yards away from the action and across the cemetery, H had never looked better. Black had always suited her and never more so than on that dull dank winter afternoon.

Even Jamie had made a decent effort, though I couldn't help feeling his white sneakers looked slightly out of place at his sister's funeral.

On the upside the Scott fan base had taken the revelations of Heather's and Jamie's incestuous relationship all in their stride. The news that they'd been fucking each other's brains out for years seemed to add yet more spice to the sordid blend of sexploitation Jamie was guilty of propagating through Facebook and other social media at every turn.

He was still on the market and the sex would be even more exotic as an ex-con, given he was also doing his sister at the same time. Surprisingly, Heather seemed okay with it all too. I was beginning to think I'd misjudged her.

In fact they looked quite the mourning couple as they walked down the lane to the chapel doors, arms wrapped tightly round one another for comfort.

They no longer cared what people thought about them. Their fan base had already forgiven them their behaviour and their number of followers was growing exponentially with every new revelation.

And that's all that counted.

I didn't understand any of it. Which was probably why I would be the eternal pauper, and they were getting rich beyond their wildest dreams.

I said my silent goodbyes and walked back to Betty.

She still loved me. It might have been something to do with the fact that I'd just treated her to that new kerbside running board she so desperately needed.

Women.